NIAGARA FONTAINE

A Meredith, Massachusetts Novel

J.A. McINTOSH

IISBN No. 978-1-7326451-1-0

DEDICATION

To Alexander, Abbigayle, and Brent
When you arrived, my life became extraordinary

SATURDAY, OCTOBER 30

Logan Memorial Hospital
100 Amanda Street
Meredith, Massachusetts
7:45 PM

Perseverance is my strongest trait. Deal with it.

I pushed open the scratched plexiglass door of the emergency department. Smelled ammonia and dried blood. I jumped out of the way as a gurney rushed past. The young woman on the gurney still had pieces of glass in her face and hair.

Once through the door, I backed against the wall and looked around, a habit I'd developed when entering a room that always brought uncertainty. I spotted Kara Salem, a social worker, in the crowd. She was short, heavy, and wore her blond hair in corkscrews. Ridiculous hairstyle, but she insisted she couldn't do anything else with it.

A nurse bustled up and I read her name tag. Important to call people by name, even if I never see them again.

"Hello, Ms. Johansson. I'm Niagara Fontaine, the attorney for the Department of Children and Families." Then I asked the same question I ask every time. "What can you tell me?"

Cecily Johansson, an RN by her name tag, played with her earring. "Don't know exactly when the man arrived at the hospital." She checked her chart. "But at about 5:30, he walked up to the emergency registration, first time we saw him, and said he didn't know what was wrong with the baby. He put the girl, four months old, on the nursing desk." Johansson flipped a page. "We found a hematoma on the side of her head and multiple other cuts and bruises. Upon examination, it appeared she had been struck with a blunt object."

Nurse Johansson looked up. "Or she hit a wall or some other fixture that didn't move. That's why I filed the report with DCF. The man who brought her in wouldn't or couldn't give any information about her injuries."

Another person spoke to the nurse. She turned to me and said, "I've got to go now. Your people are over there." She gestured vaguely toward Kara.

I followed the beacon of blond curls and pushed my way to Kara. Without a greeting, she started talking. "The child is being examined now. We should know something soon. That's the man who brought her in. Unclear if he is the father." She gestured toward a man in faded jeans and a Batman t-shirt.

The man gestured toward the woman beside him. She also wore faded clothes, without the blood stains. Another woman, in scrubs, stepped between them and linked her arm to the woman's. The man pulled on the woman's other arm.

"Let's go talk to them." I waited for Kara to move first. If this case went to court, I couldn't testify since I'm the Department's lawyer. So, Kara needed to be present for all information collection. Kara knew her part: the helpful social worker. I'm the lawyer threatening court action.

The man patted his pockets. We both stopped. He could be looking for his wallet. Or his insurance card. Or a weapon. His stained and ripped jeans were a result of hard work, not a fashion choice. His red rimmed eyes darted from side to side.

I felt Kara relax when he pulled a pack of cigarettes from the pocket of his jeans. He shook three cigarettes from the pack and re-inserted two of them. Put the third between his lips.

"Sir, you can't smoke in here," a nurse snapped.

"Ain't smoking. Just holding it in my mouth." His voice sounded like he had smoked since the age of twelve. The cigarette bobbed up and down in his mouth.

Kara stepped up beside the nurse's aide. "Sir, will you please come with us? I'm a social worker from DCF and I need to talk to you."

Moving closer to the man, I smelled something other than cigarettes. Fresh and herbal. Not breath mints, though. The sharp, woodsy fragrance of thyme.

"Why? My baby's sick. I need to stay here." The man pointed to the floor.

Kara glanced at the nurse's aide and her nametag. "My friend, Darla, will let us know if anything happens. Please come with me."

The man stared at Kara's newest friend, Darla. He chewed the end of the cigarette.

"I'm a social worker from DCF," said Kara as she guided the man from the reception area into a nearby conference room. "And this is the DCF counsel, Niagara Fontaine."

"What's DCF?" he asked.

"The Department of Children and Families," said Kara as we entered the room.

The conference room was small and utilitarian. A table with a Formica top and three plastic molded chairs. A coffee maker and a box of tissues sat on the shelf by the window.

The man stopped and looked at me. "Who the hell is she?"

"She's the lawyer from DCF. We want to talk to you."

"I don't want to talk to no lady lawyer. 'Specially a DCF lawyer." He banged his hand on the table. "I don't hafta talk to you."

In the small room, the smell of cigarettes and thyme intensified.

"No, sir, you don't have to talk to us." Kara did her best to look non-threatening. "But it might be better if you did. We have some questions."

The man banged his hand on the table a second time. "OK, 'cause I got some questions, too. You ask one, then I'll ask one."

I remained silent and waited to see the direction of the conversation.

"Sounds fair to me. What's your name?" Kara spoke directly to him.

"Abraham Lincoln. That's your one question. Now I got one, for the lady lawyer." He turned to me. "You give good head?"

I didn't respond.

"Put that in your fucking report." Mr. Lincoln left the room.

"That went well," said Kara.

I didn't respond to her either. Sometimes the lack of response was appropriate for co-workers also.

A knock on the door. It was immediately opened by a short, dark man in purple scrubs. He spoke to Kara.

"Ms. Salem, I'm Dr. Rehan. I need to talk to you about the child that was brought in."

Kara turned to the MD and introduced me. Dr. Rehan ignored me and continued.

"The child's skull fracture was in the temporal region, most likely caused by the skull hitting a blunt object. No other broken or healing bones apparent upon examination. I'll want a pediatric radiologist to do a full skeletal scan, probably more than one. No petechial hemorrhaging, no internal bleeding."

"What will the skeletal scan show you?" asked Kara.

"I'm not a pediatric radiologist. Dr. Freed is but he's not in today. A skeletal scan will show any healing fractures. I can say there are no recent breaks, but I need an expert in children and how their bones heal—it varies depending on the age of the child."

"Are you going to keep her overnight?" I needed to know where the child would be, in case further action was necessary.

"Most likely. I hope that we can do at least one skeletal survey before she is released. And we'll check again for petechial hemorrhaging—bleeding in the eyes."

My phone rang. I apologized but didn't answer it.

"Was the injury inflicted? Intentional?" I know I was asking for a legal opinion, but sometimes I got an answer.

"Most likely inflicted, but not intentional," the doctor said. "It is consistent with the mother's story of a fall."

"Are you sure?" Not the most elegant question, but I'd had a long day. "The man who brought her in seemed angry at the world. Capable of violence."

Dr. Rehan checked his chart again. "I can never be sure. There's always the possibility of child abuse. But the injuries are consistent with the mother's story." He flipped more pages. "We couldn't get a story from the father. He refused to answer any questions. All the blood is at the site of the fracture, where a child would hit her head if she fell."

My phone chimed. A text.

"I'm sorry, I have to take this." I picked up my phone. "I'm the only lawyer on call this evening."

I read the text. "Need you immediately. Dead child."

The text was from Jacque Land, my favorite social worker. Over three hundred pounds, given to interesting fashion choices, and a delightful Trinidad accent.

I concluded my business in the emergency department and left Kara Smith there.

The fastest way to my car was through the basement and to the loading dock. This time of day, nobody was down there to stop me from exiting. I took the elevator to the bottom floor.

Dead bodies were stored here, waiting for the funeral home. Everything down here was stainless steel and linoleum, making it easy to hose down and clean the area. I'd never been down here this late before. My footsteps echoed and reminded me of a slasher movie. Guess that makes me the girl in the short skirt who goes into the basement. Only no short skirt and no slasher.

I was so intent on scaring myself that I didn't realize the figure in front of me was real. Then I recognized the Batman t-shirt. He wielded a knife. Security sucked at every hospital I'd ever been in.

"Calm down. Nobody needs to get hurt." I tried to sound confident and in charge.

"You're the only one going to get hurt." He stepped toward me.

"If you hurt me, you'll have more problems than you do now. And nothing will change." I looked behind him at the door to the loading dock.

"What you looking at? Look at me. They going to take the baby away. And Trisha will blame me."

"I'll bet Trisha's worried she can't find you and wants you upstairs right now." I slid to the right, closer to the door.

"She's not doing good," he said. "She's worried about where the baby is, too."

He lowered the knife a few inches. I edged a few more steps to the right.

"Don't think about it." He pointed the knife at me. "You get on your phone and you call them upstairs and tell them not to take my baby."

"That's not my decision. I'll make a call, but I don't decide where your baby goes."

He wiped his face with the edge of the Batman shirt. Left-handed, he kept the knife in his right hand, close to me. "You're the DCF lawyer. I heard the nurse say you decide whether they go to court." As he stepped closer, I smelled tobacco and thyme.

Someone moved at the end of the corridor. He signaled me to keep talking. "I'm not going to court now. I'm here to get my car and go home." Jacque flashed through my mind. He'd be frantic that I hadn't arrived.

As if on cue, my phone rang. "That's my boss, wondering where I am, because I'm supposed to be somewhere else. Let me go and we can forget this ever happened." My phone stopped ringing.

"I don't know."

The man stepped out of one of the side rooms, closer now. He raised a gun. "Stop, security. Put down the knife."

His voice boomed through the hallway. I jumped. Batman shirt grabbed me by the jacket and turned.

"Stay back." I felt the knife against my neck. I didn't much like the idea of being a hostage. If only I could faint, become dead weight. If he tried to get me out of here, I'd fake it.

"Don't hurt her or I'll shoot."

"Come closer, I want to see you." Batman shirt tucked the knife under my chin.

"No, this is fine. I can shoot you before you can stab me." Great, an argument about speed and physics.

"I may not be able to stab you, but I can stab her before you shoot me."

"You stab her, I shoot you, you're dead anyway. And she's in a hospital and will probably survive."

"Ah, shit." I heard, rather than saw, the man drop the knife.

"Now step away from her and away from the knife," said the man with the gun. He pressed a button on the microphone attached to his uniform and requested additional security. They seemed to appear immediately.

They cuffed Batman shirt and led him away.

"Are you all right?" asked my rescuer.

"I'm fine. I'm an attorney with the Department of Children and Families and people are waiting for me at another critical site. I have to leave."

"Hospital security is going to want a statement. Police department, too. You got a card?" he asked.

We exchanged cards. His read, "Troy Higgins, Private Security" with a post office box and a phone number.

"And here's another one you might want to consider." He handed me another card, with his name, that stated he was a weapons and self-defense instructor.

"I'm not sure I need this." I tried to give the card back.

"Just think about it. Call me tomorrow to schedule an interview." He turned and left.

I went to my car and got away before the police arrived with more questions.

"Scarlett Scarletti—dumb name for a kid." State Trooper Eduardo Alvarez threw the folder on the scarred table. "And she's dead."

I caught the folder as it threatened to fall off the table. I could move fast, even after running up three flights of stairs.

Some, maybe most, of the sarcasm was because I was present at one of his crime scenes. Couldn't be helped.

"What do you want to know?" His voice held all the warmth of a New England winter.

I would mourn the child later. Now I had to put aside my emotions about the child and about Alvarez. "I want to know what happened, how Scarlett died. And I want to know where the brother and sister are. They live here, too."

"Stabbed at least eight times. Found by her sister, stuffed into a closet in the back bedroom. Dead six to eight hours. I set up my work area here in the hallway after the crime scene people cleared it. Third floor apartment is the crime scene and off limits to unauthorized personnel. You can't go in. Anything else you need to know?"

Alvarez put his hands behind his back, squared his shoulders, and looked down at me. Always thought of him as Alvarez, even when we were married. Didn't often call him Al and never Eddie.

I put my hands behind my back, squared my shoulders, and wished that I had worn heels. "Where are Scarlett's siblings? And where is my social worker?"

"The children are with Jacque Land, your social worker." He pronounced the name correctly, somewhere between Jock and Jake; not many people did. "They couldn't stay here. The lady on the second floor let them go into her apartment."

I looked past Alvarez into the kitchen. A wooden table, four chairs, a white refrigerator covered with magnets, and an avocado-colored stove with some unidentifiable substance burned onto the surface. People moved around; I heard them rather than saw them.

Alvarez looked out the window at the end of the hall. "They're removing the body in a few minutes. Don't mess up my investigation."

Not that I'd ever messed up one of his investigations. His obsession with order bordered on legendary. During our marriage, he didn't allow me to iron his uniforms because, according to him, I never did it right. But then, neither did the dry cleaner. I glanced at his pants. Creases down the front were sharp and straight.

"What are you staring at?" Alvarez's question brought me back to the situation at hand.

"Nothing. Just thinking."

"Do your thinking someplace else."

"Let's focus on the situation. Where were the other people who lived in the apartment?"

"Her sister, Amber, was in the apartment during the stabbing. Says the only other person there, other than the dead child, was the mother's boyfriend. He's being held."

"Joaquin Gonzalez? I thought he was in jail."

I saw Alvarez's face change. Eyebrows raised slightly, lips tightened. He'd figured it out. "This was your case before today? You sent the kids home to this mess?"

"I didn't know Gonzalez wasn't in jail. And I checked."

Alvarez continued. "Gonzalez is in jail. It's the old boyfriend, Jimmy Scarletti. Not Scarlett's father, but she's got his name. Did you check to see where he was?"

I hadn't. Didn't even know he was still around. "I've never met him."

"And you're not going to now. He's being taken in for questioning." Alvarez shuffled the papers in front of him.

Unlikely to get any more information from him. He wanted the social worker there, to deal with the kids, but if I never showed up, I wouldn't be missed. Just a few more minutes and a few more questions. I wanted to leave as much as he wanted me gone.

"Were you involved with these kids before today?" Alvarez seemed genuinely interested and sympathetic. He almost convinced me.

"Had the case for about three years. Haven't seen the kids in a while. They don't come to court." I tried to dig up more details. Amber was good in school; I had no memory of Scarlett. Too many children over too many years.

"I'm sorry." Alvarez did look sorry. "It must be difficult when you know the children."

I wasn't going to continue with this part of the conversation. Might start crying.

"We're still collecting information." This from Alvarez, back in his "all business" mode.

"Yes, I'll read the paperwork later." I didn't need to see the gruesome details. Reading the investigations and the autopsy report was bad enough. "Can I see my social worker and the children now?"

"I'll take you down to the woman's apartment on the second floor." He stepped back into the apartment, spoke briefly, and returned.

"By the way, it wasn't my idea to take the children downstairs. Jacque Land took them to the second-floor apartment."

Alvarez never volunteered information if it wasn't to his advantage. What was going on here?

"Is the second floor a problem?"

"You decide when you get down there."

Alvarez guided me to the outside staircase. The cold air hit me. Winter was coming. Like many New England triple-deckers, this one had an outside staircase, with landings and doors on each floor. I looked over the third-floor railing, to the street below.

A small crowd, five or six people, had gathered. A couple of people smoked cigarettes and one leaned over the crime scene tape. Across the river, the Meredith Mills brick factory loomed over the town. The town name was named Meredith, after the founder William Logan's daughter, now long dead. When I first came to town, twenty-five years ago, everybody worked at the textile mill. Now, only a few dozen employees continued to make ribbon and thread in the huge building.

As I watched, the crowd parted for the coroner's wagon. It pulled up to the house and three men pulled a gurney out of the back. Like

Scarlett might still be alive. They hurried into the house.

Alvarez put a hand on my shoulder. "It's not your brother."

I stepped away. "I know."

Alvarez stepped closer. "But each new death makes us think of previous losses."

We continued down the stairs. Alvarez didn't need to say anything else. Both deaths were my responsibility. Richard died because I wasn't paying attention and Scarlett died because I agreed to send her home.

188 Washington Street
Second Floor
Meredith, Massachusetts
11:15 PM

With Alvarez behind me, I entered the apartment on the second floor. In contrast to the crime scene on the third floor, it was immaculate, though sparsely furnished, and it smelled of disinfectant. Jacque and the children sat on a maroon couch, stuffed with some lumpy material. A recliner, the only furniture in the living room other than the couch and a huge television screen, was a mustard yellow and filled by one of the largest women I've ever seen. And I've seen many large women.

Jacque held a crying girl, Amber, on his left side and the baby, Joaquin, in his lap. The large woman in the recliner pushed a button and the footrest retracted with a sigh. She placed her hands on either armrest and struggled to her feet. Alvarez mumbled something and left the apartment.

The large black-haired woman approached me. She smelled of talcum powder.

"You're the DCF lady, ain't you?" Her breasts and arms swung from side to side as she lumbered from one foot to the other. "That kid upstairs'd still be alive if you'd listened to me. I told you, when you came to see my kids, that there was more trouble upstairs than ever was in my place. Men coming in and out and yelling and kids running the hallways and you come bother me about my kid that's not going to day care, where she doesn't have to go anyway. I tried to file a report at least four times on Bella—that's her name, the mother."

The woman produced a cell phone from one of the huge pockets on the side of her

faded dress. She shook it at me. "Each time the bitch answering the phone don't listen to me. Called it remembration or something and I was just trying to get back at Bella." She delivered this information as she stood in front of the television. She stopped to take a breath. "They took her to the police station. I got nothing against Bella. She just got bad taste in men. She lets them walk all over her. They eat her food, sleep in her bed, get her knocked up, and don't come around again. Last one goes to jail, he gets out, look what happens. And you bother me about my kids. None of THEM is dead!"

I stepped directly in front of the large woman. "Mrs...?"

"It's Cass. Melinda Cass. You know me. You got a big file on me at DCF. I go to work and can't always be home looking after my kids, but if they're alone just fifteen minutes, somebody files on me and you're crawling up my ass. Me and Dwayne both work." Melinda Cass waved her hands toward the men in the kitchen. "But somebody files and you send out an eighteen-year-old social worker who's never had kids to tell me what to do. Then she leaves and me and Dwayne still got to work."

One of the men—the tall one who looked like a cadaver—looked up from the table and moved his feet. He seemed to think better of getting up from the table and slumped back into the chair.

I seized the opportunity. "Mrs. Cass, do you know anything about what happened here this evening?"

"Know anything? Dear, I know everything. Scarlett's dead. What kind of woman names her kid Scarlett? Then she gives her kids names like Amber and Joaquin, which are better but not much. Lets their fathers beat up on her, too. I knew it was just a while before one of them'd start beating on the kids. And I reported it, I did myself. But you don't ever investigate anybody but me. Why, Ellen, across the hall, she goes out all hours of the day and night and leaves her little one screaming and last week he had a cut on his head and I seen it myself and you didn't do nothing!"

Mrs. Cass's white face filled my vision. As she got angry, every part of her moved. Her jowls, her hand, and the skin hanging under her arms. The talcum powder was scented with flowers, probably lily of the valley. I took a step back.

Mrs. Cass's ramblings were giving me a headache and I still didn't know what had happened in this building. And why the kids were in this apartment. Well, if I couldn't be of any assistance as an investigator, maybe I could help with the kids.

"Are you doing all right?" I addressed the question to Jacque. He nodded his head, like Mrs. Cass had sucked all the words out of the room and there was nothing left to say. I turned my attention to Amber, sitting next to Jacque and clutching a teddy bear that was missing a left eye.

"How are you doing, Amber?" Amber opened her mouth to speak, but the voice that I heard was that of Melinda Cass.

"Well, how do you expect the child to be doing? She heard her sister being murdered. Now, my kids never heard nothing like that. I take care of them. They don't hear nobody being murdered. No, but Amber hears the yelling and screaming and gets interviewed by the police and nobody does nothing."

"Amber heard what happened?"

Jacque's mouth opened but, again, Melinda Cass's voice drowned him out.

"Yes, she did, the poor thing. The police officer asked her questions and she said that she heard her Scarlett screaming and her father yelling. And she came down here to see me, poor thing. She knows that I can take care of children."

"Jacque, let's take these children to a safe place." I started to pick up the coats, hats, toys, and knapsacks spread around the room.

"I think that these poor children should stay with me. They know me. Why be put into foster care with strangers when they can stay with me and you can see them anytime that you want?"

Mrs. Cass tried to get a knapsack away from Jacque. "Don't you want to stay with me, honey?" Amber started to cry.

Not wanting to confront Mrs. Cass and explain that the children could not be placed in a home with an open DCF case, which certainly sounded like what she said, I did nothing. Couldn't be certain of all the facts, even after all of Mrs. Cass's words. Tried diplomacy. "Mrs. Cass, something terrible happened here tonight and we can't be sure what effect it will have on the children. They need to be in a place without bad memories. Depending on how they're doing, we may reassess the situation in a few days."

Mrs. Cass plunked her bulk down in front of Amber. "Honey, be a good girl and you can come back to see me in a few days."

"Mrs. Cass, I did not say that. Please don't make false promises to the child."

Jacque stepped between us. "Mrs. Cass, I will come to see you tomorrow. We can discuss what happened and I'll let you know how Amber and Joaquin are doing."

"See, he understands what I'm saying. I want to know about the kids."

Leave it to Jacque to diffuse the situation. At the same time, he towered over everyone and pushed the children and me out of the room. Almost made it out, too, when the door opened. Two blonds, a girl about four and a boy, maybe three years old, entered the apartment. The boy's left arm hung out of his coat at a strange angle. No adult accompanied the children.

The boy struggled to take off his coat.

Jacque knelt to help him. "Buddy, what's wrong with your arm?"

"Ain't nothing wrong with that arm. It's been like that all day." Melinda Cass grabbed for the coat. "He said it don't hurt."

Jacque positioned himself between Mrs. Cass and the boy. "How long has it been like this?"

"He don't complain about it at all. Just a bruise. He's been playing at the neighbor's, didn't come home to complain."

"How long has he been at the neighbor's house?" asked Jacque.

"Left this afternoon to play at Ginny Linnehan's house. Called to say they was going to eat there, didn't say nothing about the arm. Ginny lives a coupla doors down."

Ginny Linnehan. That sounded familiar. Her diagnosis was bipolar disorder and she put her children into foster care whenever she went into the psychiatric ward.

"Ginny Linnehan lives three or four blocks away. Where is she now? Why didn't she walk the kids home?" Jacque's voice sounded casual, not like he cared about the answer.

"She said the kids'd be home at seven. It's just a little after now. No problem." Melinda Cass's voice cracked. "Don't start your DCF stuff on me now."

The man at the table, probably Dwayne, banged his boots on the kitchen floor, dragged himself up by holding on to the edge of the table, and ambled into the living room.

"Get away from my kid. He ain't none of your business either. I'll take care of him." His voice shook the apartment walls. His speech complete, he collapsed into the recliner.

"The boy's arm is injured. I want to look at it," Jacque said.

Dwayne sank further into the chair. Six feet tall and as skinny as Melinda Cass was wide. His legs contorted around the chair legs and he pulled his long arms into his sides. Even his bushy eyebrows and hook nose shrank.

"It hung that way all day. See what goes on in this house, yet you always come after me." Melinda Cass grabbed the injured arm and attempted to lead the boy from the room. He screamed.

Dwayne got up from the chair and started toward me. No match for Melinda, who elbowed him out of the way. He roared like a bull elephant, but Melinda just screamed back at him.

"You never pay no attention to this kid. You just drink my beer and take up space in my apartment. I'll take care of this." Melinda glared up at Dwayne.

Dwayne sat down again. His feet twitched in a bizarre dance.

Trooper Alvarez opened the apartment door without knocking. "I hear yelling. Is there trouble here?" He looked at Melinda Cass, Dwayne sprawled in the chair, and then me.

"No, no problem." Jacque pulled up the blond boy's shirt sleeve. His arm showed purple and green bruises in several places. "I think his arm is broken. And these lines could be finger marks."

"Your son needs medical attention. Sir, what is your name?" I hoped Jacque had gathered names and addresses on everyone in the apartment.

"I'm Dwayne Hall. I'm taking care of these two." He gestured vaguely in the direction of the two blond children and attempted, unsuccessfully, to rise from the chair. "David and Debbie. Can't remember their last name."

"Where are the children's parents?"

"Don't got a father," said Melinda Cass. "Mother left them here twelve days ago. Don't know where she went, but she ain't been back here."

"David needs medical attention. He is not using his arm and he screamed when Mrs. Cass touched it." I went to stand next to the boy. "I'd like to take him to the Medical Center."

"I'll drive him."

"No, Mr. Hall, I think it would be better if someone else drove him."

"You dumb bitch. I didn't say anything when you was going to take Amber and Joaquin and now you want to take all of them."

Trooper Alvarez stepped in. "Sir, you are obviously under the influence of some substance." The trooper's speech was interrupted when Mr. Hall took a swing at him, missed, and collapsed on the floor.

Alvarez turned to me. "I recommend you take all four children. There's no evidence of a legal caretaker and this intoxicated alleged caretaker assaulted a police officer. You can do your investigation and sort it out tomorrow. And Mr. Hall is under arrest." He placed a call. Another trooper came in and took Hall away.

Everyone looked at me. It was my call, but Alvarez didn't usually acknowledge that. "We'll take them all. David will need to go to the hospital."

Jacque, still holding Joaquin in his arms, led Amber to the door. Alvarez picked up the blond girl and handed her to me. He picked up the blond boy himself and walked to the door.

"At least they got normal names." Melinda Cass collapsed on the couch and didn't try to stop our exit.

At last, we made it to the street. I took a deep breath of fresh air.

"I am exhausted from just listening to her." I said to Jacque. "How long were you in there with the children?"

"I've been here since about five-thirty. I called to find out how the kids were, and a state trooper answered the phone. They were going to call us anyway, so I told emergency services that I'd cover it. Cass invited me into the apartment and I needed somewhere to check the kids, so I accepted. Bad decision."

Debbie was heavy, but awake, so I put her on the ground and held her hand.

"I'm hungry," said Debbie.

"Me too," echoed Amber.

Jacque, always prepared, pulled crackers and trail mix from his car. Both girls ate crackers. The boys slept, unaware of what they missed. I was hungry, too. The girls had finished all the crackers and I hate trail mix.

Jacque transferred Joaquin, fast asleep, from his right hip to his left. "And now I've got to get David to the Medical Center and the others to foster homes. I don't think I've got enough car seats for three children, even if Amber doesn't need one."

"I've got one in my cruiser," Trooper Alvarez said.

I couldn't keep the surprise from my face when I looked at him.

He continued, "I did the safety seat training today. The regular guy was out. I haven't returned the seat yet."

After some discussion, it was decided that Jacque was going to the hospital with David. Trooper Alvarez, of course, had more pressing duties and left.

"Put the other seats in my car. I'll take the children to their foster home." Not my favorite activity at midnight, putting three children into unfamiliar car seats. It took three tries with the infant seat. Finally, we buckled the groggy children into the seats. Glad I had Jacque, who didn't think it was a problem.

On my way out of the parking lot, I decided I needed food, preferably something salty and greasy. In Meredith, Massachusetts, population 4,000, that meant the Quick Stop convenience store. It was the only place open all night.

But first, the children needed to be delivered to the foster home. Mrs. Burke, the foster mother, offered to take all three children, and she had diapers and formula. I started the car and drove past streets lined with row houses. The houses, built for the workers at the textile mills, fell into disrepair after the mills closed. When I was a child, the smell of wet wool was in the air year-round. My parents, before their deaths, told me stories about seeing wool particles in the air. I parked in front of one of the tall, narrow apartments with a tiny trimmed lawn. Mrs. Burke opened the door, came to my car and helped me unbuckle and lift the sleeping children.

We set up the pac-n-play, a modified playpen and bed, in the living room and put Joaquin in it. Amber and Debbie went directly to bed. Mrs. Burke said she had a system and she'd manage the details later. I was happy to leave her to it.

I dragged myself to the car. Still hungry, I drove to the Quick Stop. Crackers to replace the ones the girls ate, a bag of salt and vinegar chips, chocolate bars, a quart of milk, some yogurt, and a loaf of whole wheat bread, so the clerk didn't think I was a complete junk food junkie. Quick Mart made $36.64 off me that night.

SUNDAY, OCTOBER 31

1065 Main Street
Apartment 2C
Meredith, Massachusetts
1:17 AM

Finally home, I dumped the potato chips, chocolate bars, and yogurt containers on the kitchen counter. Found some strawberry protein powder, poured it into a glass, and added ice cubes. The phone rang.

"David's arm is broken. He caused more damage by using it all day. They're keeping him overnight." Jacque sounded exhausted.

"Where are you?"

"Logan Hospital. I didn't want to drive into Worcester. Figured the local hospital could set a broken arm."

Took a sip of my drink. The protein powder had been around a while. "Do you want to stay here tonight? It'll save you the drive into the city. Don't know why you want to live there anyway."

"Works for me," he replied. "Sure you want to risk your reputation by having me for the night?"

"I'll chance it. Give the neighbors something to talk about."

"Won't it just. Be there in about an hour." As usual, Jacque did not say goodbye.

The protein shake didn't do it. Started on the bag of potato chips. Salt and vinegar, brand name. Four years of therapy and all I learned was to eat exactly what I wanted or end up eating twice as much of what I didn't want but ate anyway. Not even a decent diagnosis, like an anorexic movie star. No, stuck with "ED-NOS" on every form. Eating disorder—not otherwise specified.

Put the empty chocolate wrappers, though I don't remember eating chocolate, in the trash and covered them with paper bags.

When Jacque arrived, the kitchen clock read 1:55. He flopped down into an upholstered chair.

"I could use a drink."

"I have single malt." No food, but plenty of bottles in the cabinet. "Glenlivet okay?"

"That'd be wonderful. Neat, please."

I pushed the potato chip bag and half a chocolate bar to the side. Found a reasonably clean glass, poured Jacque's drink, and handed it to him. Walked to the couch, curled my feet up under me, and gulped the protein shake.

"Girlfriend, how much you had to eat?" Jacque rubbed a tiny stain off the glass.

"You mean besides the protein shake and a banana?"

Jacque stared at me. "I've known you too long to believe that 'protein shake and a banana' shit."

"So, do you think David is going to be okay?" Now I was craving the rest of the potato chips. Damn Jacque for bringing it up.

"Don't go changing the subject. We're talking about you. How're you feeling and what've you had to eat?"

"That's none of your business."

"Tough." Jacque sipped his drink. "I'm a social worker and I'm being social."

"I've got a therapist. I don't need you."

"Yeah, you been in therapy forever and you got your stomach stapled and you're cured." Jacque wiped the glass with a napkin. "But how do you feel?"

Stomach stapling. Jacque made it sound like an office procedure, not the hell it was. Four years of therapy, binge eating, hoarding food, and then gastric bypass surgery to reduce the stomach to the size of an egg. Having to learn what and when to eat all over again. And still getting the overwhelming urges to binge when the job got to be too much.

"I don't want to talk about it."

"You never want to talk 'bout it." Jacque got up from the chair, went to the cabinet, removed a glass, washed it, and poured his drink into the new, washed glass. "You think you're responsible for sending that kid home?" He sat down again, facing me. "You in charge of the universe? Must be a tough job."

"I'm just tired. And why do you always wash my glasses, even though I give you a clean one? Alcohol kills germs."

"I prefer a clean glass, that's all." Jacque held his glass up to the light and studied it. "It isn't all or nothing, you know. You aren't responsible for everything, always."

A knock on the door interrupted the conversation.

"Who the hell is that at two am?" I walked to the door and opened it.

"Do you always answer the door without knowing who's behind it?" Alvarez walked into the room.

And stopped dead. The sight of a six-foot-two, three-hundred-pound man with a round mahogany face and wearing a Hawaiian shirt did that to you. Jacque smiled and lifted his glass.

Alvarez looked past Jacque to the liquor bottles, chip bags, and banana peels. "Have I interrupted something?"

"No, darlin', you haven't interrupted anythin'. Can I get you a drink?" Jacque managed to sound even more Caribbean when he flirted.

I realized that I wasn't the only one attracted to men in uniform. My third foster mother said it was because I looked for order in my life.

"Why are you here? And how did you get in the security door?"

Alvarez held several pieces of paper. "I thought you might want the reports from tonight. The woman in 4D let me in."

Done in by Mrs. Schmidt.

"Do you want something to eat or drink?"

"No, I'm still on duty and have to go. Can I speak to you alone?"

"Jacque is the social worker assigned to the Scarletti case. He can hear anything."

Alvarez glanced toward Jacque. "This isn't about the case. Can we just step into the hall?"

Couldn't find my keys, or my purse either. I was careful to check the door was unlocked before we went out into the hallway.

Good thing. Alvarez shut the door.

I leaned against the wall, mostly because I was too exhausted to stand. "What's the problem, Trooper Alvarez?"

"There's something wrong about this situation with Scarlett." He looked down at his boots. "More premeditated than we thought at first."

"What do you mean by premeditated?"

"I can't go into details. It's an ongoing investigation." He did his thing with his hands behind his back, looking down on me. "I just want you to be careful. Look around. Be aware of your surroundings."

"And you didn't want to say this in front of Jacque?"

"He makes me uncomfortable. I think I interest him too much."

That made me smile. "You do. And he's generally a good judge of character."

"Just be careful." Alvarez left.

I opened the door to the apartment.

Jacque sprawled in the chair. "I guess I'm not the only one interested in Trooper Alvarez. I'd say the guy was smitten with you." Jacque glanced at me. "And I wanted him for myself."

At least they weren't talking about my eating habits. "I don't think he's interested in you."

"Too bad." Jacque stood up. "But you're still avoiding the issue."

"Yes, I am." Went to the kitchen counter and checked through the Quick Stop bags. Looked around some more. "Have you seen my purse?"

"You haven't used it since I came into the room." Jacques glanced around the room. "When did you last have it?"

"I paid for my food at the Quick Stop."

"Tonight? You went to that place with the children?"

Always thinking of the children. "No, after I dropped them off." I pulled the keys from one of the bags. "Well, at least I still have the keys. I'm going to see if my purse is in the car."

Jacque shrugged. "I'll go make up my bed." He left the room.

Checked under the seats and opened the trunk. Nothing. Keys must have been in my hand when I left the convenience store, but I had no memory of putting them in a purse. Such a hassle to notify the credit card companies and get a new license. The purse also contained my bar association card, my official identification badge. Now I'd be searched by security at the courthouse and at the office. Didn't like people going through my stuff. The Quick Mart is always open. I pulled my mobile phone out of my pocket and called Jacque to tell him I was going back to the store.

Not there either.

I felt frantic. But not frantic enough to call Mrs. Burke and interrupt her settling in the children or, even worse, her sleep. Good foster parents were hard to find, so I'd call her in the morning. Besides, I had the purse at the store, after I left her place.

I parked the car, let myself into the house and poured my own glass of Glenlivet.

Contemplated the half-full bottle. Where had the scotch gone? Spied a few potato chip crumbs on the counter and ate them. Then three or four cookies. Then, to make it healthy, a banana.

I didn't feel better. In fact, I felt worse. The heartburn started just above my solar plexus and spread. Needed to move around. The problem with having a small stomach was that it filled up fast; the overflow had to go somewhere. The familiar feeling overcame me, like snakes in the throat. I couldn't keep down everything I ate. Ran for the bathroom.

When I came out, Jacque leaned against the wall.

"Are you all right? Is there anything I can do?"

"No, I feel better now. Just temporary, I guess."

"What did you have to eat? Besides the protein shake, I mean."

"Several handfuls of potato chips and a banana."

Jacque remained silent.

"Okay, a bag of chips, a few cookies, half a chocolate bar, and a banana."

"In the last ten minutes. No wonder you got sick."

"Hey, it's the first time in weeks that it's happened. I'm almost cured."

"Almost cured. You don't eat anything for hours, then you eat until you get sick. That ain't almost cured."

"I'm working on it." I ambled into Jacque's room and ran my hand over the newly made bed. "Can't find my purse either."

"Did you search the car?"

"No, I walked out into the cold night, drove to the store, and didn't look in the car."

"No need to get snippy. But for an organized person, you sure lost something important."

"Is this a listing of my faults?"

"OK, if we're making a list, let's talk about you feeling guilty about Scarlett. It's not always everything or nothing. People mess up. It took a lot of people and a lot of decisions to get Scarlett dead. But the person responsible is the one who killed her, not you." Jacque sipped his drink. "And are you responsible for losing your purse too?"

"I'm sure the purse will show up tomorrow. I didn't go that far." I smoothed out another non-existent wrinkle and looked up. "But what if it doesn't? It'll take days to replace everything in there. Bar card, license, and credit cards. I want to call the foster mother but I'm afraid to wake up the kids. At least I got my phone and my keys. What if somebody's using my credit cards right now?"

Jacque put his hand over mine. "I know, I'm on your side. And replacing lost cards can be a hassle. But don't freak out just 'cause your super organized life hits a snag. Stop awfulizing and catastrophizing."

"Awfulizing and catastrophizing?"

Jacque shrugged. "It's what my niece Genevieve calls it when somebody immediately goes to the worst possible thing. Not that it can't happen, but you use up so much energy worrying about what might happen."

"Stop being such a damn social worker."

"That's what I am. That's what I do."

Yes, and that's why I requested him on the toughest cases. And why he was my friend. "Anyway, I didn't mean to flare up at you. We okay?"

"Done. Now get out of here so I can get some sleep."

1065 Main Street
Apartment 2C
Meredith, Massachusetts
6:20 AM

Every day, I wake up between six and seven. My internal clock doesn't know it's Sunday. Never get to sleep in. Then I remembered. No purse. I'd have to go back to the store and the apartment and the hospital. And disturb Mrs. Burke and the kids. And, if I couldn't find it, then notify all the credit card companies and the bar association and the banks.

Jacque was gone. But he'd made coffee before he left. I logged on to the website of the Board of Bar Overseers. The name is a quaint reminder of three hundred or so years of Massachusetts legal history. Found places to register and renew, but I couldn't figure out how to get a replacement card. Made a list of the credit card companies I'd have to call.

The phone rang. Jacque.

"Hey." His usual greeting. A child screamed, and something hit a metal object in the background.

"Where are you?" I took another sip of coffee. It was cold. "Are you out on a call without me?"

"No, honey, I'm at home." Jacque was the youngest of eight children, and the only male. He lived with three of his sisters. "Trying to feed Joey breakfast." Joey was the youngest of his numerous nieces and nephews. About eighteen months old, if I had the right child.

"And you thought you'd call and let me in on the fun of children in the early morning?"

"Yeah, there's that. But I wanted to tell you no purse at the Washington Street address, at either the Scarletti or the Cass apartment."

"How do you know that this early in the morning?"

"Another call to the house last night. After we left, Bella, the mother, went back to the house. Was psychiatrically hospitalized early this morning.

"No, Joey, in your mouth." Another clanking sound. "Sorry, got to deal with Joey for a minute." About thirty seconds later, Jacque resumed. "Short version, new on-call supervisor sent another set of social workers to the house because of the psych call. Got there, realized the kids were already in state custody, and called me. They didn't have anything else to do, so I had them ask around about the purse. No luck."

"Could have left it in the Cass apartment." I poured a fresh cup of coffee.

"Nope. Melinda Cass was out asking questions again. That woman must stay up all night. Not in her apartment either." A sound more like a pop. "It was unlikely anyway if you had the purse at the QuikMart. Gotta go." He hung up.

Well, that left the QuikMart and the hospital and Mrs. Burke. Of course, I went to the Quick Mart after all those stops, but I'm going to check anyway. Hospital and convenience store were both open 24/7 and I had nothing better to do this morning. Smeared peanut butter on an English muffin and left the house.

Still nothing at the Quick Mart. Nobody had turned in my purse. Called Mrs. Burke; it wasn't there either. Might as well go to the hospital. With all the people coming and going there, it wasn't likely the purse was noticed or turned in. But a Good Samaritan was always a possibility.

Logan Memorial Hospital
100 Amanda Street
Meredith, Massachusetts.
9:04 AM

When I got there, I didn't recognize anyone working at the nursing station. Asked some questions and was directed to the lost and found at the front desk. Before I left the emergency department, I checked the waiting room and the conference room that we used. Nothing in either place.

Went back to the front entrance. Nobody at the desk there so early on a Sunday morning. Saw some nurses and aides walk by with Cat in the Hat hats and tiaras. Damn, it was Halloween. Forgot about that entirely. I stopped a woman in scrubs with pumpkins all over it.

"Excuse me. Can you help me with the lost and found? I left my purse here last night."

She stared at me for thirty seconds. "Did the hospital call you about it?"

"No, but I was here last night and now my purse is missing."

"If it was found, with ID, we try to call." She took a pair of glasses from her pocket and put them on. The eye frames were huge carved jack-o'-lanterns. "I'll check. Be right back."

After about ten minutes, I sat down. Maybe she just kept walking and forgot all about me. Another five minutes and I'd go looking for a receptionist or some other administrative person.

I heard someone say my name. It was the security person from last night. The one who gave me his card.

"Ms. Fontaine." He stood in front of me. "Are you here to see me?"

I stood up. "Sorry, I forgot your name." That sounded bad.

"No problem. Troy Higgins." He held out his hand.

I took it. "And you've been here all night?"

"I work a twelve-hour shift. Nine PM to nine AM." He did look tired. "I just got off work. What are you doing here?"

"In the confusion last night, I lost my purse. Trying to get someone who can locate the lost and found."

"I can do that." He walked over to the door. "Follow me. You have a better chance of recognizing your stuff than I do."

We walked down another tiled corridor, past Radiology and Oncology. Troy unlocked what looked like a janitor's closet.

It was a janitor's closet, with metal shelves holding toilet paper, disposable gloves, cleaning supplies, and all the other materials needed to clean up after dozens of sick humans crammed together. On the back wall hung half a dozen metal lockers. The end one was labeled "Lost and Found." Troy opened it and out tumbled one orange sneaker, half a dozen coats, and a pink stuffed bunny.

Troy picked up the bunny. "This is where we keep all the good stuff. Don't see a purse, but you're free to go through the locker."

It took me less than three minutes to determine that my purse was not there.

"Damn," I said. "Now I'm going to have to spend the day canceling cards and tomorrow getting a new license. Not good."

Troy stuffed everything back into the locker and slammed it. "Sorry you're going to have such a tough day." He opened the locker again, rearranged the contents, and slammed it a second time. "I'm going to the shooting range later today. Want to come with me? It'll take your mind off your problems."

"No, I don't think so." It was a bad idea. I didn't need to get involved with a security cop and didn't want to see a cop after being married to Alvarez. And guns scared the hell out of me.

"Hey, I've got to go home and get some sleep. Won't be at the range until about four this afternoon. You can get all your phone calls done first." He smiled. "You will be amazed at the feeling of control shooting a gun will give you. And it's fun."

This was such a bad idea on so many levels.

"Yes, I'll be there," I said.

Meredith Shooting Club
Coke Kiln Road
Meredith, Massachusetts
4:17 PM

It was a little after four when I pulled into the Meredith Shooting Club parking lot. I hadn't spent the entire day on the phone with idiots, but it seemed that way. Hell is trying to replace credit cards on a Sunday. Nobody knew the process, the supervisor wasn't in today, "please hold for eight minutes of the song 'Changes."

The shooting club didn't look like what I'd imagined: Visions of old men in overalls with guns broken over their arms, wandering around and spitting chew. The gravel parking lot could use some work, but the main building was well maintained, if utilitarian. A shed with double doors, like a barn, stood off to the side. Somebody'd planted pink geraniums in an old tub out front. Outdoor ranges were labeled "Handguns" and "Long Guns." The grass was mowed, and the rules of the club were posted at each station.

Several men wandered the parking lot. One was dressed as a cowboy and one as Darth Vader. I hoped he didn't shoot with his plastic helmet on; no way he could see the target.

Troy pulled into the parking lot just after me in a huge truck with shiny silver wheels. He had to jump down from the cab. He was wearing faded jeans that fit well. He came up to me and looked me up and down.

I thought I looked good. I should; I changed my outfit three times. Knew this wasn't a date, but we were going out in public and I didn't want to look like a slob. Settled on my boyfriend jeans and a stretch top. It covered everything it should, though the scoop neck did show off the beginning of my cleavage. Sandals and a red bag to match the top completed the outfit.

"Hello," said Troy. He stared at my feet.

"Hello." I looked at my feet. "Is there a problem?"

He scrunched up one half of his face and looked me in the eyes. "Guess I should've told you how to dress."

Okay, my look was casual, but everything fit and nothing was torn or faded. "What's the problem with the way I'm dressed?"

He blushed. The damn man blushed. Red started at his neck and worked its way to his hairline. "You look good," he said. "Real good." He stopped to look around; several men in the parking lot were looking at us. "But that shirt and those shoes are a problem."

One of the men, the one in the cowboy outfit, snickered. Like he should be giving fashion tips. Troy stared at them. "Go on, it's not like you didn't have this conversation with your women friends." He turned back to me. "You see, it's physics and trajectory."

"Physics and trajectory and the way I'm dressed?" Now I was really confused.

"Yeah. You're going to shoot a semi-automatic pistol. It's semi auto because it cocks automatically after every shot, so every time you pull the trigger it shoots. Until you run out of bullets." He ran his fingers through his hair.

That cleared it up.

"Do you watch cop shows or forensic shows?"

I nodded, and he went on. "Well, when the investigators get to the crime scene, they look around for casings on the ground. Every time a pistol fires, it ejects a casing to make room for the next one. It's automatic, there's no way to stop the gun from ejecting the casing."

"I've seen that on *CSI* and *Forensic Files*. They match the casings to other casings or the gun to identify what weapon fired it."

"Yeah. So, they're left after every shooting. Unless the shooter picks them up afterward."

"On TV, it's called 'policing the brass,' I think." We were fast coming to the end of my forensic knowledge. "What's that got to do with how I'm dressed?"

"Well, when the brass casing leaves the pistol, it's hot. The firing pin and the hot gases propel it down the barrel. It's a bit more complicated than that but you get the idea." Again, he combed his fingers through his hair. "When the hot brass is ejected from the gun, it often goes back toward the shooter. And if it goes down the front of your shirt or hits your bare feet, it burns and leaves a mark. And you can jump and mess up your aim." He blurted out the last two sentences, as if anxious to finish.

"So, should I go home and change my clothes?"

"No, I don't think that's necessary. We'll just deal with the shoes. I have a shirt in my truck you can wear." He reached into the back of the cab and pulled out a Spiderman t-shirt at least two sizes too large for me. Everybody went to that sale at Walmart.

"You can wear this," he said.

I had my doubts. But I was willing to give it a shot. Large and floppy, the shirt hung to my knees. We walked to the low building. Another man, this one dressed in a cowboy hat and a bolo tie, pushed forms toward us.

"I'm a member," said Troy. "And she's my guest today."

"No problem." He straightened his bolo tie. "I'll need to see your membership card and a photo ID from the lady."

"I don't have a photo ID. My purse was stolen last night."

Bolo tie looked at Troy. "You know the rules. No guests on the shooting ranges without a photo ID." He turned to me. "Miss, we have to verify everybody's ID for insurance and because it's a good idea if you're going to shoot a gun." He took the paper back that he had set in front of me. "No exceptions."

Maybe this whole thing was not meant to be. First, my clothes, now my ID. The universe telling me I shouldn't fire a gun.

"We'll do the blue guns." This from Troy.

"Okay, toy guns it is. You still got to sign a waiver." Bolo tie put another form in front of me, this one on blue paper. "Got to wear a blue ID tag and not leave the reception area or the blue room."

"Toy guns?" A vision of me with a cap gun and a bunch of nine-year-olds.

"It shoots like a real gun," said Troy. "Only it's bright blue and it shoots a laser. You get the experience without the danger."

"That sounds good." I read and signed the waiver, wondering what I was getting into.

We went into a room directly off the reception area. The walls were concrete and exposed wood, with six shooting stations. The gun was royal blue and about six inches long. Heavy for its small size. Troy told me it was several ounces lighter than a hand gun, but it felt heavier than a "toy gun." As I predicted, there were three young boys, and a man who looked like their father, in the room practicing with the toy guns. No cap pistols.

The red and white targets were calibrated to the guns. Each time a target was hit, the digital readout on the bottom added to the score. I went up to the first shooting station, gripped the gun in my right hand, and held my left below the gun.

Troy laughed. "They only do the cup and saucer stance in cop shows. First, which is your dominant eye?"

"Dominant eye? My right one, I guess. I'm right-handed."

"Probably so, but let's check. Put your hands up in front of your nose, with the thumbs meeting at the bottom and the pointer fingers meeting at the top." He stopped so I could get my fingers in position. "Now pull your fingers back to the eye that gives you the best view."

Right-eyed it was. I gripped the gun in my right hand and lined the back metal sight up between the two sights in the front.

"I'm coming up behind you," said Troy. "Always tell the shooter if you are behind them. Easier on everybody. Now take your left hand and put it on the pistol grip also."

I had both hands around the grip and stood facing the target. I fired. Hit the outer rim of the target. A ten showed up on the digital readout.

"Good. The gun fits you. If you can't get both hands on the grip or one hand is behind the slide, the gun is too small. If the gun is too big or heavy, you can't control it. You'll just have to experiment to get the right one. Now try again." I fired three more shots. Missed three times.

"Don't try so hard. Breathe out when you fire." Troy was trying to be helpful, but it didn't make me any less nervous. One of the boys in the room came up to stand next to Troy.

"Hey, mister, can you help me like you help her? My dad is busy with my little brothers."

The blond kid topped out at four feet. Troy smiled at him.

"No problem, be right there. My friend will probably do better with me not looking over her shoulder." And he left to help the kid.

I pretended to study my gun while I watched him. Patient to a fault, he went over the same stance and rules with the kid at least half a dozen times. And the kid did get better. So did I. By the time our session was over, I was hitting the target three times out of four.

We were walking back out to the truck when I realized I didn't want this day to end yet. "You want to get some burgers and beer?" I asked. "I know a place about fifteen minutes from here."

Burger Barn
Old Main Street
Meredith, Massachusetts
6:40 PM

We ended up at the Burger Barn drinking local beer and eating burgers with Gouda and onions. While waiting for the food, we talked about the weather and the hassles of replacing everything from my purse. When the food arrived, I realized how hungry I was and how great the burger tasted.

"You were really good with that kid. Patient with all his questions." I dragged a French fry through the ketchup. Loved ketchup all over the fries.

"Yeah, I miss my kids."

"You have children?" Not what I had pictured. Working twelve-hour shifts at a job that couldn't pay that well. Not my image of a family man.

"Two; a girl, Andrea, and a boy, Andrew. Haven't seen them in a while, though."

"You don't live with them?" Most likely divorced. Or separated and all the craziness that implied. "Where do they live?"

"With their mother," Troy said.

"Why don't you see them?" I took a sip of my Otter River beer. "You don't have to tell me, but you did bring it up." Took another sip. "Hazard of telling things to a lawyer."

"My ex-wife took off with my kids about a year ago. Dropped off the grid. I've almost found them a few times but then she took them out of the country."

"I'm sorry."

"Yeah, me too. I move around a lot, take crap jobs, to follow them. Heard they came to New England. I just got here a few weeks ago. That's why I'm doing the graveyard shift."

"Any leads on where they are?"

"A few. I'm following up." He put his hands on the table. "Can we talk about something else?"

"Okay, how do you like working at the hospital?"

We made small talk while we finished the burgers.

As we walked to the parking lot, Troy said, "Sorry I cut you off about my kids. It's complicated and I don't like thinking about it.

"Not a problem. I hope it works out for you."

I am not going to get involved with a cop. Even a security guard. I learned my lesson. But he did look great in his jeans. I gave him back his shirt, got in my car, and I was on my way.

I was definitely going to take his shooting class.

The good feelings didn't last. As I drove, I thought about everything I needed to accomplish tomorrow. Replace my license and bar card. To the Registry of Motor Vehicles at 9 AM, then calls to the Board of Bar Overseers. Then the rest of the day will be about Scarlett's siblings and the custody hearings.

I parked my car. It was a little after eight, dark on this October night. The light bulb over the entry to the door had burned out and I fumbled with my keys. The inside hallway was well lit and deserted. I climbed the stairs, humming to myself. "I Can't Help Falling in Love With You."

I threw the keys on the table.

"Now, what's your problem?" Eduardo Alvarez was sprawled across the chair that Jacque had occupied last night. Alvarez did a better sprawl.

1065 Main Street
Apartment 2C
Meredith, Massachusetts
8:16 PM

I glanced back toward the hall. The door was locked when I arrived and locked behind me.

"What the hell? You don't live here anymore." I was more annoyed than intimidated by Alvarez. "You have no right to break into my house."

"I didn't break in, I have a key. I need to talk to you. Tonight," he said.

I needed to get that key back.

"What crap. Go talk to Tiffany or Brittany or whatever her name is. And leave the key on your way out."

"I'm here on official business. And her name was Arlena."

"And you just decided to let yourself in?"

Alvarez leaned back in the chair. "It couldn't wait until the morning. I'm here about missing children."

"Missing children? What children are missing?"

"Children in DCF custody. All over the state." Alvarez stood up. "And you may be in danger, too."

"How am I in danger?"

What really brought him here tonight? Was he having me followed? Whatever, he was leaving.

"Just hear me out." Alvarez put his hands out in front of him, palms up. "This is important."

"So is my sleep. Be quick."

"Twenty-six children involved with DCF have gone missing in the last six months. Not lost in the bureaucracy but missing without a trace. No hair, no clothing, no forensic evidence at all. And four of them turned up dead. Scarlett is the fifth."

"Missing children? Why haven't I heard about this? Seems like it would make headlines."

"The children were from fourteen different families all over the state. None of the kids were in DCF custody when they disappeared, but all of them had been involved with DCF." Alvarez ticked off each point on his fingers, as if I were slow to follow along.

"And you figured it out and kept it to yourself?"

"I didn't keep it to myself. I told my commanding officer. Just can't figure out why it happened and what it means."

"Why Scarlett? She isn't missing. She was killed at home."

"She was missing. For six weeks last summer."

Alvarez was right. I'd forgotten. Scarlett's mother took off with her and Amber and returned shortly before Joaquin was born. Said she had been on vacation, but details were sparse.

"And you think the disappearance and the murder are connected?" I still found it hard to believe Alvarez. "Why haven't I heard about this?"

"It gets worse." Alvarez was in full cop mode now. "The twenty-six children were from fourteen different families and each family had at least one child under the age of two. And none of the children under two have ever been found. The only exception is the Scarlettis. And Bella was seven months pregnant when she took off with the kids."

"You're not listening to me." As if that were a new event in my life. "Why are you the only one that knows about this? Or are the cops keeping it a secret?"

"It's no secret, all the evidence just came together. Three DCF attorneys have asked questions about the disappearances. One was in a serious car accident."

"You mean Lydia Avery? I work with her. She's in the hospital. Who are the other two?"

"Susan Thomlinson, from Brockton, left a note on her desk saying she couldn't do this job anymore. Brian with a hyphenated last name, also from Brockton, went on his honeymoon and said he wasn't coming back to work."

"I don't know either of them. Don't have much to do with that office."

"That's the problem," said Alvarez. "It took a while to recognize a pattern. DCF doesn't routinely do follow-up on closed cases and each attorney just asked about something strange they saw. Nobody had the full picture."

Alvarez seemed sincere, but the disappearances might be explained. The married guy could be really into his marriage, or moved to be near his spouse, and some people just couldn't do this job.

"What does Lydia say? I'm sure somebody has questioned her."

"She's not saying anything. Her story is that she fell asleep at the wheel."

"So you have nothing."

"We have twenty-six missing children," he said.

"Why haven't I heard about this before today? Missing children are generally in the news."

He flipped through a file on my coffee table. "That's the interesting part. Kids have disappeared from every part of the state. Over two hundred fifty towns in Massachusetts, more than twenty DCF offices. The children are involved with DCF but not in foster care. All the missing kids were with their families. One family was vacationing in Vermont."

"How do you know about this? How come you're the only one to put it together?"

"I didn't before Scarlett's death. Only started looking afterward. This is what I found."

"What are you going to do now?"

"I'm going to investigate. All the forensic evidence points to the boyfriend, Scarletti, as Scarlett's killer. But I think there's a bigger problem. But I just don't know how Scarlett's murder fits into it."

"What do you want me to do?" He always wanted something.

"Niagara, you know I always want what's best for you. I want to make sure you're okay. I'd like you to go see Lydia. See if you can get anything from her."

"And report it back to you."

Alvarez straightened his jacket. "That's the idea." He put his hand on my shoulder. "And take care of yourself. I don't want to lose you."

Alvarez moved past me to the door.

"Leave the key."

He dropped it on the table on his way out.

"And get that light outside fixed." He always had the last word.

MONDAY, NOVEMBER 1

Department of Children and Families Area Office
One Gold Street
Meredith, Massachusetts
9:17 AM

When I walked in, a young man stood in my office. Tall and skinny, with skin the color of café au lait, he shifted from foot to foot. Whoever let him into my office unsupervised was going to hear from me.

"I'm Amir Alcindor," he said. He put out his hand.

"Niagara Fontaine." We shook hands. "Can I help you?"

"Jacque Land told me to wait here for you." He spun the ring on his finger, the only jewelry he wore.

"Why did Jacque tell you to come here?"

"I'm your new intern," he said. "To do copying and stuff."

"You in college?" He didn't look old enough.

"No."

"Technical School?"

"No."

"We can play twenty questions, or you can tell me why you're here," I said.

He spun the ring faster.

I took off my coat, hung it up, and sat in my chair behind the desk. "Sit down and tell me why you're here and what Jacque said."

"I'm your intern," he repeated. "I got to do community service and Jacque said to come see you."

"How old are you?"

"You're not supposed to ask that," he said. "I'm nineteen."

"Okay, let me ask a question another way. Are you still in school with some of the kids in state custody? We have a lot of confidential information here."

"I got my GED. Jacque said to tell you I can keep my mouth shut."

I leaned back in my chair. I'd ask Jacque about this as soon as I saw him. "You got any paperwork about your internship?"

Amir pulled several sheets of ivory paper from his back pocket and laid them on the desk. I looked them over and they appeared to be standard forms for community service.

"I'll start you out on making copies. The copy machine is just outside my door, so you make the copies and bring them back. No reading the paperwork, no wandering the halls. We'll discuss this again after I talk to Jacque."

"What you want me to copy?" he asked.

"A set of 51As and 51Bs. I need five sets of them and each set must have all the pages. Count them to make sure they are all the same. Then bring them back to me."

"What's a 51A and a 51B?"

He didn't need to know all the terms to make copies, but he was here to learn.

"Some people, like police officers, teachers, and social workers, are required to file reports of suspected child abuse. Some people just do it because they're worried about a child and some people do it for spite. The report of suspected abuse or neglect is called a '51A report' because who files and how they file are in the Massachusetts General Laws at Chapter 119, section 51A. That's how the Department gets involved in a case."

"So, I could file a report if I wanted to?"

"Yes, anybody can do it." I put the pile of papers in front of him.

"How do you know if they're telling the truth or just screwing around?"

"The Department checks into that. The person getting the report makes phone calls. If it seems legitimate, we send out investigators. The investigators then make a longer report, called a 51B report."

"Because that's the section of the law that says you have to make a report." Amir picked up the stack of papers. "Do I need to read the law to know how this works?"

"No, it probably wouldn't help. The law just says what we must do, not how we do it. We can also take custody of a child without going to court. That's another set of paperwork. Feel free to ask questions but remember everybody here has deadlines and may not be able to sit down and go over things with you."

"Well, thanks for taking the time." Amir brought his right hand to his forehead in salute. "I'll get to copying."

Kara Salem appeared in the office door.

"Sorry I'm late." Kara came into my office with her file case flung over her shoulder, her purse dangling on her wrist, and her hands occupied with coffee and a sack. "Actually, do we have to do this now? It's not like it's going to make any difference. I've testified dozens of times."

I watched as Kara settled into her chair, took a sip of her coffee, and opened the Dunkin Donuts sack. Kara took out a bagel and bit into it. Didn't have any to share.

"This case is different. Everyone will be watching. A child died."

Kara put her bagel down and wiped her fingers on the napkin provided. "You didn't seem to care about the Miller kids. They're at risk, too."

I admired a person who ate so slowly and deliberately. Never mastered it. And the girl at the drive-up window never remembered to give me napkins. Maybe if I looked like Kara I'd get better service. Though Kara didn't look her best just now. In a child, I'd call it pouting. And I'm doing anything not to have to think about the dead child.

"Miller children? They're not on until this afternoon. Though I won't be surprised if the judge sends them home. We're here to prepare for the Scarletti hearing." I plunked the voluminous file in front of her. "Let's get started."

Kara wasn't finished yet. "How can you forget about the kids as soon as you leave the courtroom? From one case to another, just items to cross off on your to-do list."

Kara sounded remarkably like Jacque in her analysis. No, Jacque didn't discuss me with other social workers.

"The best way we can protect the Scarletti children is to be prepared."

Kara sighed. "I know. And I want to do well. Just, sometimes, it seems like I'm not making a difference. And, besides, Jacque has most of the information on Bella's children."

"You collected the paperwork. I hoped Jacque would be here too, but he went to pick up Amber for her interview."

"Yeah, I know." Kara took another tiny bite of her bagel. "And I need to get through my bitchy stage. Sorry I took it out on you. I know you're trying to do your best, too."

We spent the next forty-five minutes going over the case file. Kara interviewed the mother, Bella, yesterday. The police didn't let her talk to Jimmy Scarletti in jail, but Kara managed to collect a sizable number of police reports. Scarlett had fourteen stab wounds. Amazingly, none of them was fatal. She was manually strangled to death by someone with large hands. Probably not a woman. The only people in the apartment, other than Scarlett, were Jimmy Scarletti, her mother's boyfriend, and her sister, Amber. Scarletti wasn't talking and Amber wasn't clear about what she'd heard.

"Nobody in the apartment downstairs claimed to know anything." Kara finished her report. "I've been assigned to do a comprehensive assessment on the family. Melinda Cass grilled the police on whether she could get custody of the children and pointed out, at least a dozen times, that she had reported Bella in the past and got no response.

"And I'm still concerned about the Miller children, especially if the judge sends them home this afternoon."

Kara left the office.

In my office, while I waited for Jacque, I called the Board of Bar Overseers about a replacement for my bar card. Only took a few minutes and I got instructions about how to replace or renew the card online. I felt I had accomplished something, so I called VISA again. I was on hold for eighteen minutes when Jacque appeared. He wandered into my office and put a pile of papers on my desk. The papers included copies of microfiche files, battered and yellow sheets, and some recent computer printouts. It looked ready for the shredder, but I knew better than to make such an assumption with Jacque.

I picked up the papers. "What are these?"

"Jimmy Scarletti's record. Goes back thirty years to when he was a juvenile. Didn't realize he was so much older than Bella."

"Anything interesting?" I knew that he'd read it before he gave it to me.

"Man will do most anything for money. He got stopped for running a stop sign about six months ago, cop found several grams of cocaine on him. He did sixty days for that. But, before that bust, he laid low for two or three years. Back six years ago, he pled out to a series of burglaries. Makes you wonder what he was doing these last few years."

"Maybe he got better at staying away from the cops."

Jacque shook his head. "Nope. He was doing something we ain't figured out yet.

Amir appeared at the door, nodded to Jacque, put some papers on my desk, and left.

"I see you met the new intern," said Jacque. "Thought you could use some help."

"So, you decided my intern should be a nineteen-year-old kid doing community service?"

"How'd you pick up on that so quick?"

"Old fashioned investigative work," I said. "I asked him."

Jacque picked files off a chair and sat down. "Amir's a good kid. Needs some work. He can copy and get coffee and run errands."

"Can he keep his mouth shut? Some of these files are on kids not much younger than he is."

Jacque leaned forward, putting his elbows on my desk. "He can keep his mouth shut. He's been hanging around with a gang, needs to get away."

"That makes me feel better." The sarcasm was lost on Jacque.

Barbara, the office secretary, came into my office and placed a stack of files on my desk.

"I got to go," said Jacque. "Amber is in the waiting room with Kara. We need to be at the District Attorney's office at 11:00. I'm interviewing Amber for the video. Are you planning on being there?"

"Yes, I'll walk over with you. Just give me a minute."

Jacque left, and Barbara went to follow him.

"Just a minute, Barbara." I flipped through the top few files. "These aren't mine."

"Are now. Lydia Avery was in a car accident on the way back from vacation. She's at the Quinsigamond Medical Center. By the way, I'm taking a collection for her. Ten dollars if you're interested.

"She's not critical but she won't be in for a few weeks. Broken leg and broken pelvis. Her cases have been reassigned. These are yours. I've tried to reassign them to the attorney who is scheduled to be in court the same date but couldn't always get it right. Top four cases are on for tomorrow."

I recalled my conversation with Alvarez and his statements about Lydia's connections with the missing children and how he wanted me to speak with her. "How did you find out about Lydia? Can she have visitors?"

"She called in yesterday, said she wouldn't be in and why. She sounded good, considering what happened to her. The Medical Center said she could have visitors. It will cheer her up."

I wasn't thinking of cheering up Lydia. I wanted the update on her cases and to check Alvarez's story. But, I'd do my best to be cheery. I handed Barbara a ten-dollar bill.

Office of the District Attorney
Five Gold Street
Meredith, Massachusetts
11:15 AM

Jacque, Amber, and I walked across the shared parking lot to the District Attorney's office. None of us talked on the three-minute walk. We were greeted by Dierdre Ball, one of the assistant district attorneys assigned to the juvenile unit.

She knelt to Amber's level. "How are you doing today?"

Amber didn't say anything.

"My name is Dierdre. What's yours?"

"Amber Scarletti."

"Amber, do you want to see what we do here in my office?" said Dierdre.

Amber nodded.

"Let's go into this room." Dierdre led the way and Amber and Jacque followed her into the room. I waited by the door.

The room was about twelve feet by twelve feet and somebody had put some effort into making it comfortable for children. Spongebob SquarePants and some anime figures decorated the walls. In the center was a large table at kid height, with a selection of kid-size and adult-size chairs. All were in shades of blue and orange. Stuffed animals and dolls lined a shelf on the wall.

Amber stood in the middle of the room.

"This is where you and Jacque will talk," said Dierdre. "You can sit at the table and talk. You can keep a stuffed animal or a doll with you if you want to. What kind of animal do you like?"

Amber went over to the table. "Jacque will need to sit in a big chair."

Jacque went to stand next to her. "Yes, and you'll get the littler chair."

"Okay," said Amber.

"But first I've got to show you the other room," Dierdre continued. "See this big mirror."

Amber went up to the mirror and put her hand on it.

"Now let's go to the other side." We all followed Dierdre out of the room and into the room next door.

This room was smaller with a filing cabinet, some black boxes, and a camera on a tripod.

"While you're talking to Jacque, I will be in here," explained Dierdre. "This camera will be taking pictures of you and Jacque."

Amber walked up to this side of the mirror and put her hand on it. She turned to face Jacque and said, "I've got to go to the bathroom."

Jacque took Amber to the child-size bathroom and we stood in the hall, waiting for her to return.

"I heard that you're the best at this," Dierdre said to Jacque when they returned. "Let's see what you can do."

Amber and Jacque went into the larger room and sat at the table. Jacque put crayons and paper in front of her.

"Amber, how old are you?"

"Eight." Amber pushed away the paper and crayon. "I don't do crayons. You have magic markers?"

"Let me see." Jacque took down the box of drawing supplies. I knew Amber was six years old and so did Jacque. "What grade are you in?"

"Second. We got magic markers at school."

"You do? What do you draw?" He extracted several colored pencils from the box. "Will these do?"

"Not magic markers, but OK. I draw anything."

"Why don't you draw me a picture."

Amber made several small circles on the paper in front of her.

"What are you drawing?"

"Circles." Amber drew several more. "You want me to draw Scarlett? Mama said you wanted that."

Jacque looked at the drawings. He needed to proceed carefully. But the child brought up the topic. He pushed ahead.

"Can you draw me a picture of what happened?"

"No."

"Why not?"

"I didn't see nothing."

"Nothing at all?"

"Nope. Nothing." She picked up the sheet of paper with circles on it and held it in front of her. She jabbed the paper with the pencil, ripping the corner off.

"Did you hear anything?"

Amber picked up a green pencil and jabbed it toward Jacque. "Scarlett and Daddy fighting. Saying bad things."

"What bad things?"

"Don't know. Just heard yelling."

"If you just heard yelling, how did you know they were saying bad things?"

Amber jabbed at the paper until it completely shredded. "Yelling is bad things. I'm not 'sposed to yell."

Jacque scooped up the shredded paper with the circles on it and put it in his bag. Amber pushed aside the other papers on the table, took out a red crayon, and drew circles on the tabletop.

"Amber, please don't draw on the table. Here's a piece of paper."

Jacque placed a clean, white sheet of paper in front of her. She ripped it to shreds and threw it on the floor. Then she continued to draw circles on the tabletop. Jacque moved his chair over, put his large hand over hers, and removed the crayon.

"Don't wanna talk no more. Can I eat?" She looked at the table, not at Jacque.

"Can we talk some more? Where was your mother while this was going on?"

"Don't wanna talk. I'm hungry. Can I see my brother?"

Amber left the room. Jacque followed her.

The interview was over.

I was late getting to the courthouse. Jacque took Amber back to the foster home, so he was going to be even later.

When I got to the courthouse, a uniformed police officer stood outside the entrance to the parking lot, waving people past. I pulled up beside him and ran my window down.

"I'm the attorney for the Department of Children and Families. I have cases on for 2:00 PM."

"Nobody in or out of the courthouse or the parking lot. Move on."

I went a few hundred feet up the street. Someone was pulling out of a space in front of the school and I parked there. I got out of the car and called my office.

"Department of Children and Families, Legal Division. How may I direct your call?"

"Barbara, it's Niagara. I'm at the courthouse and they won't let me in."

"Yeah, we just turned on the television. There's a gunman in the courthouse. Or there was. They're not sure where he is right now. About two dozen people are being kept in the judge's lobby for their own protection."

"Where's the gunman?"

"Don't know. But there are at least three social workers in the courthouse." The rest of Barbara's speech was drowned out by a news helicopter directly over my head.

"Barbara, I'll call you later." I disconnected the call and brought the news feed up on my phone.

I looked around and saw attorneys Warner, Plane, and a third person I recognized but couldn't name sitting on the wall in front of the school. I joined them.

"Looks like they got the gunman," said Warner.

Several police officers were in a huddle on the front steps of the courthouse. A man, about forty, was face down on the steps. While we watched, he was handcuffed and pulled to his feet.

"What happened?" I asked.

"Some guy wanted to see the judge," said Warner. "Brought a gun into the courthouse."

"How'd he get a gun through the metal detector?" asked Plane.

"Don't know," said Warner. "Just repeating what they said on the news."

"Anybody get hurt?" I asked.

"Don't think so," Warner replied. "Didn't see anybody in the ambulance."

We watched the officers put the man in a cruiser and drive away. The ambulance remained parked in the lot.

"I'm going to see what's going on." Attorney Plane slid off the wall and walked to the police officer, still at the entrance to the parking lot.

He returned within a few minutes. "Officer says they need to clear the building. Looks like just one gunman, no casualties, but they want to be sure."

We waited on the wall in front of the school. I imagined a scene with a gunman as chaotic and loud. No sound other than the news helicopter, and everybody was just waiting around for something to happen. I was cold. The sun was shining but it was the first day of November. I'd almost decided to go sit in my car when the officer started waving cars into the parking lot.

"Looks like we can go back in," I said.

We walked to the courthouse and entered the front door. We turned right, toward the attorney's and employee's line through the metal detector.

"Put your bags on the conveyor belt and take off any belts, keys, or other metal items." This from the court officer at the metal detector.

"We're attorneys," said Warner and walked through.

The court officer stopped her on the other side. "Everybody goes through the metal detector today. No exceptions."

I looked around the rotunda of the courthouse. Didn't see anything suspicious, but my guard was up today.

Attorney Warner went through the detector three times before it stopped buzzing. The court officer confiscated her nail file and her mace.

"Pick it up on your way out. Have a nice day," said the court officer.

Worcester Juvenile Court, Meredith Session
118 Main Street
Meredith, Massachusetts
3:37 PM

I went directly to the courtroom where Judge Hartwell was waiting.

"Case number 01M0045. Matter of the Miller children. Attorney Fontaine for the Department of Children and Families, Attorney Paoletti for mother, Attorney Warner for children. Mother is also present."

Judge Hartwell looked at the parties. "Counselors, we are here today for my decision in this matter." The judge adjusted her robe and reached for a single piece of paper. "For the reasons set forth in my written decision, I am returning the children to mother's custody. Please make arrangements to have them returned by five PM today. That is all."

I felt my fingers tighten on my briefcase. Though the decision was not unexpected, I wasn't giving up. "Please note the Department's objection to the court's ruling. Please also accept the Department's Motion for Reconsideration."

The judge looked briefly at the motion before denying it.

"The Department also asks that this court stay its order to return the children home until the appeal may be heard."

"Notice of appeal is at your discretion. Stay is denied. The children are going home today." The judge looked over her glasses at the attorneys before her.

My knuckles were white. I deliberately tried to relax and started packing up my things. "Thank you, Your Honor."

I left the courtroom. Kara Salem, the social worker on the Miller case, followed close behind. "What happened? Why did she return the children home?"

"Let's get out of the hallway. See if we can find a conference room." As usual, every conference room in the juvenile court was filled. We went into a less-traveled hallway.

"The judge didn't believe that the mother knew the children were being abused. With her boyfriend in jail, the judge thinks that the children are safe at home."

"What does the judge think mother was doing while Sam was hitting the kids? It's not that big an apartment." Kara rocked back and forth from one leg to the other.

"She believes mother. It doesn't matter that we don't." I hated these discussions with social workers after a lost court case. Especially one that I should have won. What was Judge Hartwell thinking, sending kids back home to a mother who took in every loser off the street?

A court officer, distinguishable by his white shirt, utility belt, and swagger, rounded the corner. "Attorney Fontaine, we need you in the courtroom for an emergency filing."

"Do I have to go get the children now? Can we talk about this first?" Kara twirled her hair around her finger.

"We can talk about it. But the order says that the children must be home by five. That's less than two hours from now. If you want to wait, I can talk to you after I finish this session. But you'd better call and have somebody prepare the children."

"No, I think that I should do it. Can't we stop this?"

"The judge denied the stay. The children are going home. We can talk about it after." I hoped to avoid that discussion. Hated dissecting my failures. Hated even more defending a system I knew was flawed.

"We can't let the children go home. Look what happened when you let Scarlett go home. She's dead."

I tried to keep my face neutral. I considered it an advantage that the DCF attorneys were not generally in the spotlight. But that didn't stop the blame from my co-workers and the blame I put on myself. Scarlett went home under an agreement I made. The Miller children were going home under court order. Neither guaranteed safety.

"I'm sorry, I know that you're sensitive about it. But it's dangerous to send kids home if their mother can't or won't protect them," Kara's voice went up an octave.

"We are not going to discuss Scarlett. The judge has issued an order. We can obey it or appeal it. Until the appeal is finished, the order stands. The children will go home today." The enforcer role didn't come naturally to me. But, as the Regional Counsel said, the defense attorney can afford to be passionate, but the prosecutor had to be unemotional and calculating.

"Don't you care about these children?" Kara's voice grew loud and shrill.

"Yes, I care." I gritted my teeth. "But I also believe that the system works. I know you have a gut feeling that these kids are in trouble, but the judge isn't convinced. We don't have enough evidence." I turned to go. Even a cold and calculating prosecutor had her limits.

"What if the foster mother doesn't return the children?"

I placed myself directly in front of Kara. "The children are going home. We do not hide children."

Unbidden memories surfaced of a foster mother who took the children, not home, but to her attorney's office where they held a press conference. I knew Kara remembered too. "Your only conversation with the foster mother will be about when and where the children are returned. She won't hide the children without encouragement from you. Don't give her any." I tried to feel as authoritative as I sounded.

A distinctly male voice interrupted the conversation. "Attorney Fontaine, you are wanted in the courtroom." The court officer returned to fetch me. "Follow me now."

I took a deep breath and followed him into Judge Ramos' courtroom. I put aside my feelings and did the job. Maybe Jacque was right, people and their feelings messed up my job and my world. Especially my own feelings.

Despite Barbara's positive spin, Lydia was drawn and gray, though she did seem happy to see me. Late in the day, maybe she was just tired. I was, and I only felt slightly guilty for deliberately arriving near the end of visiting hours.

"I picked one of the more painful ways to get out of work." Lydia smiled, and I responded in kind. "So, you inherited my cases for tomorrow? Lucky you, I don't have much on until later in the month."

We spent thirty minutes going over the cases. Some pretrial conferences. Lydia had already prepared the paperwork. They only needed trial dates and a motion to continue a date because a lawyer was in trial in another court.

And the Hall children, removed the same night that Scarlett was killed. I was familiar with that case from the removal with Jacque, knew the parents had not been located, so we spent only a few minutes on the matter. By some quirk of court scheduling, the Hall custody hearing was scheduled to be heard the day before the Scarletti siblings.

As I prepared to leave, I looked around the hospital room. We still hadn't discussed Alvarez's suspicions, and I was tired.

The room held a bed, a nightstand, and some tubes and wires I didn't want to know the use for. There was an empty second bed. No cards, no flowers, no mementos. "Can I bring you anything? Food, hairbrush?"

"Thanks, no. I don't have any family here, but the hospital has supplied the essentials and the nurses lent me some books to read. I really don't feel like eating."

"What happened to you? How did you end up here?"

Lydia shifted in the bed. "Fell asleep at the wheel."

"This ever happened before?" Yes, I realized how foolish that sounded. "Not the accident, of course. But you making a long drive and getting tired."

"No. I'd been driving six hours. Went to visit my family in Pennsylvania. I do it a few times a year, always drive. Guess I was really tired. Drove off the road into a tree."

"Ouch. What's broken?"

"Broke my leg and cracked my pelvis. Got some interesting bruises, too." Lydia picked at the sheet. "I'd rather not talk about this anymore."

I stepped back. Lydia looked grayer than she had just twenty minutes ago. And much more tense.

"Rumor in the office is that somebody else may have caused the accident."

Lydia adjusted her IV. "Who? I was the only one there."

Lydia's monotone made me even more suspicious. Very rehearsed, very mechanical.

"Was something wrong with your car? Do you think it's connected to a case you're working on?"

"No, my car is fine. It was my fault. Why all the questions?"

I debated whether to ask her directly about the missing children. But I didn't have the chance. The intercom crackled, signaling the end of visiting hours.

"Please send the nurse in on your way out. I need pain medication."

I checked out the morphine drip and the needle running into Lydia's arm. It was unlikely she was getting additional pain medication. But I did as she asked.

On the way out, I asked, "Okay if I call you if I have any questions?"

Lydia looked terrified.

TUESDAY, NOVEMBER 2

Department of Children and Families Legal Office
Legal Division
45 Maple Street
Worcester, Massachusetts
8:00 AM

Determined to catch up on my paperwork and data entry, I was in my office at 8:00 am. More messages waited. Another call from Attorney Plane; I'd have to pull that file and figure out what was going on. There had been several calls from other attorneys about cases on later this week. Also, several emails from social workers about birth certificates, paternity testing, and scheduling adoptions. Nothing that couldn't wait.

As I can type faster than I can write, in addition to having control issues, I preferred to enter the data myself. After about an hour, I finished notes about yesterday's court events and the trips to the Scarletti house.

The phone rang.

"Is this Niagara Fontaine?"

Unfamiliar voice.

"Yes, may I help you?"

"Ms. Fontaine, this is Lois Smith at Meredith Mills. I'm calling about your purse."

"I lost my purse."

"I know. I have it."

Two days too late. Why was the purse at the mill, over two miles from the Quick Stop? "Where did you find the purse?"

"At the mill. In the water wheel."

A prank call. Maybe someone picked up my purse and just wanted to give me a hard time.

"Water wheel?" I asked.

"Yes, the purse was in the river and picked up in the water wheel. We still have one, though the factory runs on oil these days."

The woman seemed sincere. I made an appointment to pick up the purse after lunch. Then I called the Meredith Mills to confirm that Lois Smith worked there.

Without knocking, Barbara, our department secretary, entered my office. "You're late for the meeting." She waved her hands.

"What meeting?"

"This one." She thrust a paper into my hand.

Community Adoption Party blazed across the top of the multi-colored flyer.

"Adoption Party?" I asked.

"Don't play dumb with me." Barbara crossed her arms. "You know what an adoption party is. Kids freed for adoption go to a party and meet couples and other people wanting to adopt. This one's scheduled for a month from now."

"I hate adoption parties. Kids get all dressed up, are paraded around. Their hopes are raised and, if they don't find an adoptive family, they act out for a month. Don't blame them, I'd be pissed too."

"But it's your turn to sit in on the meeting and placate the sponsors. I'll bet you haven't even sent out feelers for kids, either."

"I did. Just haven't heard back." I took a few steps past my desk, then stopped. "Is everyone else here?"

"Yup. In Conference Room A. And I've done some follow-up on kids." Barbara smiled. "I'll see what I can get for you."

I pulled open the door to the conference room. Barbara hadn't exaggerated. Everyone was at the meeting: Judge Hartwell; Damon Davis, the General Counsel for the Department of Children and Families; Evelyn McMasters, the Regional Counsel and my immediate boss, Andrew Ames; and Ames's assistant, Amanda Simmons. Ames almost never came to meetings. He owned a string of dry cleaners and bankrolled adoption recruitment services from a private foundation. He sent memos and expected them to be executed immediately while he bragged about all he did to community groups and to television cameras. Double damn.

"Niagara, take a seat." McMasters pulled out the seat next to her. "We were just getting to the list of children going to the adoption party. Perfect timing."

I ambled to the coffee pot and took my time adding cream. Still couldn't come up with a decent excuse for not having a list. That left telling the truth.

Ames gave me a reprieve.

"I'd like to discuss the marketing for this and future adoption parties." Ames placed a thick leather folder on the table. Everyone looked at him. He had the money, he set the agenda. "My firm will highlight selected children in our ads. I could interview older children and play with the younger ones." He opened the folder. "I have some storyboards and ideas."

As Ames droned on, I looked through the papers. Nothing that could pass as a list of children. Ames made me uncomfortable. Children did get adopted through his ads and parties, but every commercial also included his face and a testimony for his dry-cleaning business. He even tried to get his commercials dubbed "Public Service Announcements" so he didn't have to pay for them.

Barbara entered the room. Ames kept talking. Barbara put more paper in front of me and left without saying a word. I flipped the pages and found a list of twenty children freed for adoption and ready to go to an adoption party. A hand-written note that invitations would be sent by the end of the day was included.

She deserved a raise. Not that it was in my power to get her one. But maybe some flowers or a gift certificate.

Ames droned on.

Department of Children and Families
Legal Division
45 Maple Street
Worcester, Massachusetts
1:10 PM

At 1:10, I called the downstairs deli and ordered lunch. Soup and half a chicken salad sandwich. Standard lunch working in the office. Also standard, every attorney in the office ate lunch together. Don't remember how it started, but it now qualified as tradition. I looked forward to the break from the work day, even if we often discussed cases.

At the deli counter, Sasha was pouring coffee, putting up sandwiches, and calling most customers by name.

"Hi, Niagara." Sasha beamed like she had been waiting all day for me. "The usual? Need coffee today?"

"No thanks. Somebody finally restocked the soda machine."

"Then it's $8.95 plus tax."

I handed over the money, turned to go, and walked into a wall of muscle.

I looked up into Troy's blue eyes. I felt a tremor go through me. He was just touching my arm. This was bad.

"You here for lunch?" I asked.

"Yeah, I had an errand downtown this morning. About my kids."

"Is everything okay?"

"Yeah," he said again. "I gotta go. See you tonight in class." He left without any food.

That was strange. Maybe he was just distracted.

When I arrived at the lunch room, Evan Howard and Lee Chu were already there.

Tim Ianella joined us, though he'd already eaten. As usual, he shared his noontime lunch with Andy Paoletti, an attorney who'd left the Department five weeks ago to take an associate position in a multi-name law firm in the bank tower. Andy's brother, Gerard, was still waiting for a return call from me. I briefly considered postponing lunch and calling him now, but the chance to hear how

Andy was doing made me stay.

Tim launched right in. "So, I arrive at the twelfth floor of the bank tower and announce myself. Nice digs, you can see the whole of downtown out of the floor to ceiling windows. But I feel like the poor relative, waiting for Andy. Guys walking by with suits that cost more than my car." Tim paused for a drink. "Not that I notice guys and their suits, but sometimes it's obvious."

"So, anyway, I'm a few minutes early because court ended, and I had nowhere else to go. Andy comes out, says give him about fifteen more minutes and I can wait in the conference room. He asks if I want coffee and says one of the secretaries will bring it to me."

Several lawyers put down their lunches to listen to him. He continued. "So, I'm sitting in the conference room and in comes a secretary with a silver coffee service and real cups. Far from our world of Styrofoam and Mr. Coffee. And everything is on a glass tray, which I'm afraid I'm going to break. So, I meet the secretary at the door, which is about nineteen yards from where I'm sitting, and tell her I'll just keep the coffee cup, she can take the tray and the rest of it back."

Tim paused for dramatic effect before he continued. "And she says to me, 'But, sir, I can't give you coffee without a tray. It's against the rules.'

"Now, I think she's pulling my leg and I say 'What, you got rules about coffee?' like it's the funniest thing I ever heard. And she says, of course they do. The coffee must be on a tray, in case it spills or drips over, so it doesn't get on the carpet. Mr. Wallace is very particular about his carpets.

"So, I ask her who Mr. Wallace is. Now she looks at me like I just asked did she murder her mother and says that Mr. Wallace is the managing partner. He wrote the four-page memo on how to serve coffee. Four pages on serving coffee! And I come from a place where we're lucky if we have coffee that don't eat through the machine. I know I'm in the wrong place."

"So, what did you do?" Lee Chu played the straight person on a regular basis.

"I didn't have to do anything. Andy arrived and I hot-footed it out of there."

"How is Andy doing?" Lee again, right on cue.

"He's making piles of money. But he's running ragged. He said he billed fifty-four hours last week. That's hours billed, not including administrative stuff."

A silence followed, while everyone there contemplated job opportunities.

Evan Howard joined the discussion. "So, Niagara, I hear you were part of the fun with the gunman yesterday."

With everything else that was going on, it took me a moment to figure out what he was referring to. "Never actually got into the courthouse with the gunman. But I saw him on the front steps." I peeled the banana in my hand. "I guess he was after the judge."

"I hear he was after his kids," said Evan.

"He did say his kids were missing. What is that about?" Lina asked.

Tim jumped in again. "He said his girlfriend had them adopted and he can't find them. Was really pissed. They called in all the court officers to assist."

"Were you there yesterday? I didn't see you," I said.

Tim grinned. "I just got to the courthouse when all hell broke loose. I was on the security officer's phone, making a call. They couldn't call out until I got off the phone. Now there's a new rule, we can't use that phone anymore."

"So, what happened?" I asked again.

"So, the thing about the phone is going to be a real problem. Mobile phones don't always work in the courthouse and now I'll have to carry quarters for the pay phone."

I raised my voice. "Get off the issue of the phone. Just carry a calling card like I do. What happened to the gunman? How did he get a gun into the courthouse anyway?"

Evan answered. "I hear it was brought in by an attorney. Tracy Christensen."

I shook my head. "Tracy? Why would she do something dumb like that?"

Once again, Tim had a story. "I hear she fell hard for the guy.

His name is Banks. Got him into rehab and helped him get a job when he got out."

"Wait a minute," Lee waved her hands. "How did she meet him?"

"Defended him on an OUI. That's Operating Under the Influence for those of you who never practiced criminal law. Quite an education, criminal law. Who's who in perversion."

"One story at a time." Lee's hands were moving in a circular motion. "What happened with Tracy Christensen?"

"Like I said, she fell for him. Heard she got caught straddling him in the attorney conference room at the jail."

"That's just a rumor," said Evan. "She knows the jail has cameras and guards can walk in on you anytime. Tracy'd have to be an idiot to do that."

"Like bringing a gun into court is a smart move?" I couldn't help the sarcasm. But I still found it hard to believe. "Are they sure she brought in the gun?"

"That's what I heard." Tim continued his story, "Anyway, he completes a 28-day program and Tracy has him work in her office. He gets all fired up about his kids getting adopted. And Tracy helps him, best she can. Not much she could do."

"But why a gun?" Evan asked.

"All this is just rumors floating around the courthouse," said Lee. "None of it may be true."

Tim nodded. "And we know how stories go."

I did know how stories go. Stories about Alvarez and I had circulated for years. That I gave him information I collected on parents. Sometimes true, but the details were exaggerated. On the other hand, there were stories that I was withholding information from him.

Tracy Christensen wasn't a friend of mine, but I had seen her around the courthouse and wondered how she was reacting to the stories. And how much was true.

Meredith Mills
One Logan Place
Meredith, Massachusetts
2:15 PM

I finished lunch and drove to the Meredith Mills to retrieve my purse. Not much had changed at the mill. Same gravel parking lot, same hard benches in the office waiting room.

Ten years ago, I'd sat on these same hard benches and filled out an employment application after my first husband, Brian, had lost four jobs in six months. Until now, I'd thought my memories of this office as depressing reflected my mood at that time. Wrong. The office was depressing, and the benches were hard.

Lois Smith had tightly curled hair that was briefly in style about thirty years ago. Maybe she was reliving her glory days before marriage and children and this depressing job. Don't remember her from my job application days, but I could imagine her sitting here for decades.

She sat at a wooden desk behind a Plexiglas partition. She handed me a stained, battered purse. "Sorry about the condition. As I told you, it went through the water wheel and it really chews things up."

"So there actually is a water wheel here?" I turned the mangled leather in my hands.

"Yes, the mill was originally powered by water. A canal still runs under Main Street." Ms. Smith might do tours in her spare time. "Built the mill around the water wheel. It's too expensive to move, though it isn't used anymore."

I opened the purse. My credit cards and driver's license were still inside, though unreadable. No money though, and I had at least twenty dollars with me that night. I checked the back compartment; they took my emergency twenty-dollar bill too.

I thanked Lois Smith and left.

Meredith Shooting Club
Coke Kiln Road
Meredith, Massachusetts
7:05 PM

The gun that I now knew was a revolver didn't come apart. First lesson at the Shooting Club and I was all thumbs. We started at 6:00 PM with roll call and a lecture on safety. Troy Higgins taught the class with an older woman, Elspeth Darrow. She was just barely five feet tall, had iron gray hair and a hesitant manner that didn't seem to fit with a shooting instructor. But she took apart the revolver and put it back together in seconds. She wanted me to do the same.

I needed to separate the top from the bottom of the revolver to clean it. I couldn't get the barrel off the frame. I think that's the correct naming, but everything seemed to have left my head. I got the round cylinder out, checked for bullets left in the gun, and stopped. No clue what to do next.

Elspeth came up beside me. She took the gun and had it apart in 6.9 seconds. "You've got to do it like you mean it," she said.

The blue gun on Sunday was fun, but this one could kill somebody. I breathed deeply, stopped shaking, and dismantled the damn thing. Then waited while the other fifteen people in the class did the same.

During the rest of the class, we discussed parts of revolvers, pistols, rifles, and shotguns. Like cars, there is a make and model for every consumer and no two models seem to look or be the same. Rim fire and center fire. Shells and cartridges. Overwhelming.

"No live fire tonight," announced Troy after another half hour.

Damn. Troy splits us into four groups of four, one for each shooting station at the indoor range. Two groups would meet before class on Tuesdays and Fridays, and the other would meet after class on those days. I sign up for the late class.

As I gathered my coat and brand-new textbook, Troy approached me.

"Want to grab a drink with me?" he asked.

I thought about it for all of twenty seconds. "Sure. Where?"

"Downtown," he said. "A friend of mine is playing at the Blind

Pig."

"Okay, but I turn into a pumpkin at midnight." I smiled. "Seriously, I can't stay late, I have to be in court tomorrow."

"That's fine," Troy said. "It's the Blind Pig. Even the bar is closed by eleven."

The Blind Pig
Exchange Street
Meredith, Massachusetts
8:25 PM

The place was three quarters full when we got there. Troy had connections. A table was reserved for us in the second row. The waiter introduced himself, poured water, placed wine glasses and menus, and left.

I looked around. "Lots of people for a Tuesday night. The sign at the door said the entertainment is Tom St. Hilaire. He the guy you know?"

"Yeah, Tom's been writing songs in Nashville." Troy picked up the menu. "From Massachusetts to Tennessee. Now he's back and trying to make a name for himself."

We checked out the specials and ordered local beers named after local landmarks.

Troy took a sip of the Tom Swamp beer. "Not bad," Troy placed the glass on the table. "I heard a lawyer brought the gun into the courthouse. She wasn't searched, just walked right in."

"How'd you hear about that?"

"I'm the local shooting instructor. Hear lots of things having to do with guns. Especially at the courthouse." Troy took another sip. "This is good. So, did she walk right in with the gun?"

"Could be," I said. "I'm known at the courthouse and get waved through the metal detector daily. It's considered a sign of status not to have to empty your pockets and take off your coat."

Troy stared at the table. "I heard she was involved with the guy. Defended him on an OUI, got him cleaned up, and they became an item."

"That's what I heard, too." I shook my head. "I just find it hard to believe."

"Maybe she believes he's innocent and is trying to get clean. Maybe she loves him."

"I'd never jeopardize my career and my freedom for anybody. Especially if I knew that he was a convicted criminal. How can she trust him?"

"Trust isn't always rational. When you're in love, you see beyond the obvious," said Troy.

"But he was convicted. How could she think that she was smarter than a jury? I know the jury system has problems, but six people didn't believe him. Why should she?"

"Spoken by someone who has never been in love, I guess."

I stared past Troy's left shoulder and said nothing.

"Have I touched a nerve? What do you have against romantics?"

"My parents were romantics, gave me this name. Do you know how tough it is for a thirteen-year-old named Niagara?"

"I think Niagara is a beautiful name. How did you get it?"

"I was named after my parents' honeymoon spot. I was born nine months and five days after they were married." I continued to stare past Troy's shoulder.

Troy dug into the appetizers with obvious enthusiasm. I didn't pay much attention when he ordered them, but they did look good. Potato skins and cheese. Chicken quesadilla bites. I watched him. His hands were broad but long, an interesting combination. And, judging by the way he held the fork, a light touch. He handed me a plate. I put a potato skin and two chicken bites on it. I tried not to think about eating disorders.

Troy went back to eating. He cut each piece of chicken and brought it to his mouth with his left hand, slowly and deliberately.

The house lights went up. A tall man dressed in jeans and a black button-down shirt appeared on the stage. A voice announced Tom St. Hilaire.

"The entertainment arrives." Troy leaned back in his chair. "I think you'll like him."

St. Hilaire sat on the tiny stage, alone with a guitar and a stool. That was all he needed. He played songs he composed himself, current Nashville favorites, and older songs. I found myself singing along to "You are My Sunshine" and assorted Garth Brooks tunes. When the stage went dark, over an hour had passed.

"You look like you enjoyed that." Troy leaned back in his chair.

"It was great. I haven't been out like this in quite a while."

Troy waved over a waiter. "How about another beer?"

I hesitated.

"How can you resist Moose River beer? Or let Hal pick out one for you."

Hal, the waiter, said, "You can't go wrong with Moose River. Or, if you like hoppy beers, Tom Swamp."

How had Troy remembered the waiter's name? I never remember the names of waiters.

Troy took my hand. "I just don't want the night to end. It's been a while since I had a good time laughing and eating with a friend. Please say something."

He wanted a friend. No pressure, just someone to laugh and be with. I smiled. "I think Tom is very talented. And I'd like a Moose River."

A shadow loomed over the table. Tom St. Hilaire stood there, as if he were expected.

"Tom, good to see you. Join us." Troy stood up and shook hands. "Niagara, this is Tom St. Hilaire. Tom, my friend, Niagara Fontaine."

Tom and Troy sat down.

"Troy said he might bring you here," Tom said. "Glad he did."

"He didn't tell me about you. How do you two know each other?"

The two men launched into a convoluted story about high school, cars that didn't start, and being forced to take piano lessons. Growing up together in Georgia.

I realized that Troy valued his friend. I leaned back in my chair and watched them. Our beers arrived.

Tom turned to me. "So, what kind of foolish things has Troy talked you into?"

"Foolish things?"

"Yes, Troy has a way of talking people into doing things they never knew they wanted to do."

I wiped the rim of my glass. "Like what?"

Tom laughed. Put his head back and laughed out loud. "Watch out, Troy, you've got a cautious one here."

"I got her to come out with me and listen to you, didn't I?"

"That you did. But now I have to go and get ready for a second half. Need to wow them again."

I liked this man. "And I'm sure you will wow them. You're very talented."

"Lots of talented people out there." Tom got up to leave. "But to make it, you have to be talented and lucky. I'm working on the second part." He left.

"You have interesting friends," I said.

"I plan it that way. Though Tom is one of my few friends who didn't turn out to be a cop or a criminal. Music made a difference for him."

"Most of your friends are cops or criminals?"

"Yup. You are a new experience for me. Branching out into lawyers. Maybe I'll even make friends with a social worker or janitor."

"I happen to like social workers and janitors. How come so many cops?"

He talked about wanting to be a cop all his life, about coming from a family of cops, and about being married before and how his wife had left him when he was in the Army.

When we left the restaurant, Troy put his arm around my shoulders. The conversation ceased but that didn't seem to be a problem.

We separated in the parking lot, each going to our own cars.

At the car door, I took out my keys. "Thank you for a wonderful evening. I enjoyed myself."

I gave him a peck on the cheek, got in my car, and drove away.

Damn, what had I done now? I was not going to fall for another cop, or security officer, or whatever the hell he was. My life was finally going the way that I wanted. Not another cop, or wanna-be cop, with all the control and authority issues, to tell me what to do and say and think in the interests of protecting me. I even managed to survive the rest of the evening without gorging myself.

WEDNESDAY, NOVEMBER 3

Department of Children and Families Area Office
One Gold Street
Meredith, Massachusetts

It was my third cup of coffee in the last two hours. Never tasted battery acid, but the comparison seemed valid. Though I needed it, I was now just jittery. Jacque had gone to pick up Bella Scarletti, Scarlett's mother, and I decided to take a walk before he arrived.

It was a cold, clear November day. Slightly chilly, but I'd grabbed my jacket on the way out. I started down the sidewalk for a quick survey of the building. Just past the smokers, I heard a voice call my name. I turned to see a tall, thin woman with a mess of black hair.

"Can I talk to you?" she asked. "Do you know who I am?"

"You're Tracy Christensen," I said. All the things I'd heard about her in the last few days rushed into my head. I didn't say them. "You're a lawyer."

She smiled. "Not for long," she said. "Guess you heard about my friend, George Banks, and my problems with the court."

Interesting way to put it. "Yeah, I did."

"Now I have to wear this." Tracy lifted the leg of her tailored pantsuit to reveal an ELMO, also known as an electronic monitoring device. "Just got a few minutes before I have to report to the courthouse." She smoothed her pant leg over the anklet so that it didn't show.

"I need to talk to you. Because you're the DCF attorney that took George's kids. And he needs to know where they went. George Banks, I mean." This all came out as one sentence, as if Tracy were racing to get to the courthouse before the monitor knew she was missing.

"I don't remember a George Banks," I replied. "I've had almost a thousand cases over the last five years."

"Please look into it. He can't. He's in jail. And I can't, because of this." She waved in the general direction of her ankle. "He says his kids were taken out of state and adopted. I've got to go."

She left.

When I returned to the conference room, Jacque was there with

Bella Scarletti, Scarlett's mother. Bella looked worse than I felt. Her eyes, red and swollen, didn't focus, her hair stuck to her cheeks and her clothing smelled like urine and cigarettes.

"Sit down, Mrs. Scarletti."

Bella slumped into the straight-back chair. Her emaciated frame took up less space than a pile of laundry.

"Would you like something to drink?" Jacque said in his best host voice. He always got to be the "good cop."

"I'm good."

She obviously wasn't.

"Bella, we have some questions to ask you about the night Scarlett died." First rule of the good cop: call the person by her first name.

"I don't know what happened. Wasn't there."

Jacque opened the folder in front of him. "But you knew Jimmy was in the house?"

"When I got the kids back, you told me Joaquin couldn't live with me. Didn't say nothing about Jimmy."

"You agreed to you and the kids in the apartment. We thought Jimmy was in jail."

"Can't help it if you're too stupid to figure out where he is."

I strained to keep my mouth shut; I had promised to stay out of the conversation. Jacque, an expert interviewer, had established a relationship with Bella over the last few months. He could get more out of her.

"Where he is now is in jail."

"'Cause he killed my Scarlett." Bella cried softly.

Jacque handed her the box of tissues. "Yes, he did. Because you let him in the house."

Bella continued to cry. She blew her nose.

"Don't you think I'm feeling bad about it?" Bella addressed the wall. "But I love Jimmy and he's been like a father to all my kids."

Jacque and I refrained from comment.

"I wasn't sure I wanted another baby. Thought about an abortion. Jimmy talked me out of it. That's how much he wanted this child. Man wants a child that bad, he's got to love me."

The silence piled up in the corners of the room.

"But I need to think about my other kids now. Don't have any money to bury Scarlett. Need to go to work. My kids can stay with Melinda Cass. She'll take good care of them. They know her."

I decided it was time for a reality check. "Mrs. Scarletti, the children are in the custody of the state. They can't stay with Mrs. Cass."

"Sure, they can. Just give them back to me. We'll grieve together. That's best for all of us. I didn't kill Scarlett."

Seemed like Mrs. Scarletti had talked to her therapist that morning. I suspected the words coming out now weren't Bella's, but the therapist's. She wasn't a woman who would spontaneously think about grieving with Mrs. Cass.

"Bella, you let Jimmy into your apartment. We can't give the children back to you unless the judge says so." I stated the obvious.

"So, let's go see the judge." Bella looked around the conference room as if the judge were hidden there.

"We'll see him on Friday." Once again, Jacque calmed the waters. "And you can ask him to place the children with you or with Melinda."

"Okay, that's what I'll do. I'll call my lawyer and get the kids." Bella rummaged through her purse and pulled out a pack of generic cigarettes. "But now I need a smoke and to go to the funeral home." She rose, put the unlit cigarette between her lips, and left the office.

"What do you know about Melinda Cass?" I asked Jacque as I picked up the folder labeled "Cass" to check for myself.

"She's got an open case here and her partner, Dwayne Hall, has two convictions for possession with intent to sell," Jacque responded. "Cocaine and heroin."

"So, are you suggesting we place the children with her?"

"Hell, no."

Worcester Juvenile Court, Meredith Session
118 Main Street
Meredith, Massachusetts

Despite an early start, I was late for court. I rushed up the courthouse steps, past the usual hangers-on.

"Bitch—you took my kids." I looked at the disheveled woman, in her Marilyn Manson t-shirt and shorts. I didn't recognize her at all.

At the clerk's office, Martha, the case coordinator, looked up from the fax machine. "Rough day today. The judge is running behind schedule." She handed me a file folder.

I thumbed through the contents. "Do you have a certified copy of the decree on the Campbell children?"

"Thought I gave that to you a few weeks ago," said Martha.

"You did, but it disappeared from my office. Nobody knows anything about it."

"Things disappear from your office on a regular basis?" asked Martha.

"You know they don't." I shook my head. "We have multiple systems for keeping track of everything but, in the last two weeks, some papers have been misplaced. Nothing I can't replace.

"When I started this job, nobody told me that a third of my time'd be chasing paper, getting people to sign papers, and making copies of papers people have already signed."

"Our legal system runs on paper." Martha tapped her computer. "Even now that we're completely computerized. Did Troy Higgins get in touch with you?"

I continued flipping through the file. "I didn't know he was looking for me."

"Called a few times. Said it was important. But not as important as the judge, so get moving."

Juvenile Court was held on the second floor and I counted the stairs as exercise. The woman with the Marilyn Manson t-shirt, who had yelled at me on the steps, leaned against the wall. About forty other people crowded the narrow corridor.

The questions started as soon as I stepped into the corridor.

"I'm here for the Demartino case. I have a client coming in at 3:00. Will I be out in time?"

Glanced at my watch. 2:15. "Not likely, the judge is running behind."

"I'm here on the Clark matter. Do you know who my lawyer is?"

"Check in downstairs in the clerk's office. They'll be able to tell you."

"About the McGuiness matter. Do you plan to send the children home in the near future?"

I was taken aback by that one. "Is McGuiness on today? I don't have it on my list."

"No, it's on for the thirtieth. I just wanted to check because I don't often get a chance to talk to you in court." The well-dressed man grinned.

"I haven't even reviewed the cases for two weeks away. I'll check and get back to you." I walked away before he decided to go through his entire case list. I thought I saw Higgins in the hallway. Only a few weeks, but I kept seeing him everywhere. Back to work.

"What's on the list for today?" The court officer was the last in line. "I need to be out of here at 4:30 and there's no overtime money left for a replacement."

The judge was not yet on the bench when I entered the court room, the court officer at my heels.

"Niagara, I have some stuff for you." The clerk handed me yet another file folder.

"Good stuff or bad stuff?"

"Reports and investigations. The Clark investigation is in there. It came in about a half hour ago."

"The Clark case is on for today." Again, the watch; it read 2:38. "Forty minutes ago." I sat down to read.

The court officer came in, followed by the judge with his robe still unfastened.

"How many children do we still have in lockup?" The questions started before the judge sat down. "Can we get them out of here soon?"

"I'm ready on all three of them." The assistant district attorney pulled out his own stack of file folders. "We can start with Manny Rivera."

The judge looked at me. "We will need to finish the delinquencies in lockup before we get to you. About forty-five minutes."

I went back out into the hallway where the questions started again.

"What about the Hall children? This should be an easy one. The mother is willing to waive the custody hearing; she's going to rehab." Attorney Vale stood before me.

The Hall children, Debbie and David, were removed the night of Scarlett's death. Jacque and Lydia had given me the basic facts a few days ago.

The court officer came out of the courtroom. "Attorney Fontaine, do you have a quick matter?"

"Hall is quick, and everyone is here. We can do it now." Attorney Vale answered for me. "Sorry, did you have another case ready to go?"

"No." I pushed past her into the courtroom.

At the Commonwealth's table, I took out my calendar and the day's list. "The Commonwealth calls the Hall case." I did a last review of the file as the participants came into the room.

Priscilla Hayden, the sessions clerk, called the case. "Your honor, this is the matter of the Care and Protection of the Hall children. Attorney Fontaine for the Commonwealth, Attorney Vale for the mother. Attorney King for the children. The matter is on today for preliminary hearing."

The judge started his questions. "Have the children been identified?"

I checked my notes. "The children were identified at the filing."

The judge continued with his checklist. "Are the parents indigent? Do they qualify for appointed counsel?"

The probation officer stood. Probation was supposed to interview each parent before the hearing. Parents arrived late, needed to meet with their attorneys; probation officers had other duties, and it often didn't get done. But the probation officer had the interview sheet and it looked like it was filled out. "Mother is eligible for appointed counsel. Father is not. "

"Who are the people in the courtroom?" The parents needed to be served official papers to inform them of the consequences of the hearing. The judge looked around the courtroom. I glanced behind me for the first time. Troy Higgins was sitting on the bench. I hadn't imagined seeing him earlier. But what was he doing here?

Higgins stood. "I am Troy Higgins, the father of the children."

I felt the cold start in my feet and creep up my legs. The father of the children? Must have heard incorrectly. But Judge Ramos continued through the preliminary questions.

"Mr. Higgins, do you intend to get your own attorney? You are not eligible for appointed counsel."

"Yes, Your Honor, I would like an attorney. But I need some time to hire one."

I hadn't been mistaken. I took a deep breath. The cold spread, even though the conversation was one that I had heard dozens, if not hundreds, of times.

"We'll need another date anyway," Vale broke in. "Mother is waiving the preliminary hearing, but she may want the matter reviewed when she gets out of rehab."

"Is that correct?"

"Yes." My voice was small and weak.

"OK, let's pick another date."

The business of the court continued while I waited for my body to thaw. I remembered a conversation about children he did not see. He hadn't thought it important enough to share that they were here and involved with the court.

"Your Honor, I don't want him here when you talk about my kids." This statement from a washed-out blond sitting several places away from Troy.

"Ma'am, who are you?" asked Judge Ramos.

"I'm Margaret Wallace, mother of the children. And I don't want Troy to have anything to do with my kids."

"I'm sorry, you don't get to make that decision," said the judge. "He is the father of the children."

"He hasn't seen them in a year," continued Margaret. "And I

don't think he's the father." She glared at Troy.

Troy stood, "Your Honor, we were married when the children were born. I am their father."

Rick King, the children's attorney, knew his job. "Your Honor, I request paternity testing for my client. If Mr. Higgins will make himself available."

"Of course," said Troy.

The judge ordered paternity testing. My fingers thawed out enough so that I could pick up a pen. What a fool I was. Our relationship, if it could stand that title, was all in my head. I automatically entered the date in my calendar and left the courtroom.

Troy stopped me in the hallway. "Niagara, can I talk to you?"

I didn't want to talk to him, I didn't think I could form words. I needed to review the file, see how I had missed such an important piece of information. How I had so ignored the personal implications.

"Ms. Fontaine, can I talk to you about the McGuiness case?" The grinning attorney was back. "Can we do it now?"

"Of course, we can. Let's go into a conference room." I pushed past Troy, anxious to discuss the McGuiness case, though I hadn't reviewed it and it was not on the list for two weeks.

Anything to avoid Troy.

I spent the rest of the afternoon hiding in my office. I didn't answer the phone; all calls went to voicemail. I shuffled papers around my desk. A little after four, Barbara knocked on my door.

"Come in." Not what I wanted to say.

"You've got a call on line 2," announced Barbara. "Says it's important."

"Don't want to talk to him." At least not for another twenty-four hours. That may be enough time to regain my sanity.

"Isn't a him." Barbara pointed to the blinking light. "It's Kara Salem, and you're still the on-call attorney until 4:30." While that was technically true, when the DCF office was open, all matters were handled there. And Barbara knew that.

I picked up the phone.

"There's a problem about the Miller children," Kara said.

"They did get home to mother, didn't they?" If they didn't, I was going to kill Kara.

"Yes, they went home. But now they're missing."

"Define missing."

"Missing, as in I can't find them. I went to check on them about 2 PM and the neighbor said that mother had packed the car and the kids and left. She doesn't know where they went."

"Mother has custody of the children now. She can take them anywhere she wants to. Maybe they went on a trip or to a relative's home."

"Yeah, I guess so. I just have a bad feeling. We shouldn't have sent the kids home. There could be another perv in the house."

"We didn't send the kids home, the judge ordered it. I guess a call to the police station won't be out of order. See if they report any accidents or missing children. Let me know if you get any more information."

"I'll make the calls right away and get back to you. Let's hope they come home soon."

Kara had been doing this job for four years and it wasn't like her to be so hinky about a missing child. "If I'm not here, just call back later. I'm going out for food, but it shouldn't take long."

I hung up the phoneIt rang again. It seemed that half the state had this number.

If I left now, I could make the bakery before it closed. It was Wednesday and the special was chocolate brownies.

My caller ID indicated it was Troy. Hell, the entire day sucked, I might as well talk to him now. I picked up the phone.

"Let me explain." He started right in, no greeting. Guess he thought I'd hang up on him. I considered it.

"Niagara, are you there?"

"Yeah. I'm here." I agreed to talk to him. I didn't agree to make it easy on him.

"Margaret showed up out of nowhere. She said the state took the kids. I tried to call you. I don't know what to do."

"You should talk it over with your lawyer."

"Niagara, I want to talk to you. I want your help."

"I don't think I can help you. I'm the attorney for the other side. It's a conflict." I was saying all the right things, but I felt the cold again. Started in my feet and worked its way up.

"Just for a few minutes. In a public place. You're already signed up for my gun safety class tomorrow night. Can we meet after the class? Just for a few minutes?"

"Just for a few minutes. And we can't discuss the court case."

"See you then. I appreciate anything you can do for me."

Probably couldn't do anything, now I really needed to stop at the bakery for chocolate brownies.

I bought four.

THURSDAY, NOVEMBER 4

Worcester Juvenile Court
Meredith Session
118 Main Street
Meredith, Massachusetts
10:20 AM

Already I had a headache and the session hadn't even started yet. Good news was that I'd drawn Judge Hartwell for the day. She was known for being calm and fair. And she was a mother and didn't suffer fools. Bad news was that my headache had a name: Harry Waters, the social worker for the Bartolli family.

He wasn't even a lawyer. Fifteen years ago, Harry Waters had arrived at my foster home and announced that he was my new social worker. When he arrived, I had a decent relationship with my foster mother, Mrs. W. I called her that because she had an unpronounceable Polish last name. I was going to school every day and had discovered I had a way with words.

Waters had other plans. Under the guise of "being realistic" he enrolled me in vocational school because, he said, there was no way to pay for college.

Some people thrive in vocational school, but I was clumsy and slow and hated it. When transportation to the school became a problem, he pulled me out of Mrs. W's and sent me to a group home nearer the school. Cut off from my friends and school, I escaped by getting pregnant and marrying Brian. Of course, the story was not quite that logical and linear. By the time I miscarried, Waters was no longer my social worker and I had another path to follow.

Now Waters was a colleague. Twenty-five years as a social worker. No promotions, no supervisor position. His lack of progress in the Department wasn't because he was dedicated to direct care. It was because he was obnoxious. He hadn't changed. His most recent assignment was this case.

Mrs. Bartolli, a widow with two children, had moved in with a sex offender. A Level 3 sex offender, one that the Commonwealth of Massachusetts found to be at a high level of dangerousness and highly likely to reoffend.

"We need to get those kids out of the house. They're only nineteen months and three months old. He could be abusing them every day, and nobody'd know." Waters stood ramrod straight, blessing the masses with his insight.

Once again, I found myself defending a system I knew was flawed. "We have no evidence that she or her boyfriend did anything to these kids. He's not convicted as a pedophile. All his offenses were assault and battery on a child over the age of fourteen."

"Then mother should be scared. And keeping him out of the house."

Couldn't argue with the logic. But what I knew and what I could prove were drastically different.

Before I got to the Bartolli case, the only one on for hearing today, I proceeded through the rest of the day's cases. During all court matters, my thoughts drifted toward Troy and my inability to help him. Mixed in with feelings of helplessness and anger was a nagging feeling that I may not have the full story.

Waters spent the time talking to various people and making notes on his tablet. I concentrated on my work and tried to push other thoughts from my mind.

The court officer called the Bartolli case. Though I harbored doubts about the strength of the case, we went forward with the preliminary custody hearing. Let the judge decide. Waters had presented an affidavit and got custody on a temporary basis, but now, just two days later, I needed to convince a judge to continue custody. No evidence of the sex offender harming these children, but I kept pounding away at his registration status and that the Commonwealth of Massachusetts had found him to be dangerous and at a high risk to reoffend.

After my opening statement, I called Harry Waters to the stand. I could do the direct examination by rote and so could he.

"Please state your name and occupation for the court."

"Harry Waters, investigator for the Department of Children and Families."

"In your duties as an investigator for the Department, were you assigned case responsibility for the Bartolli family?"

Waters knew the drill also. "Yes, I was assigned the investigation on October 29 of this year."

I walked Waters through receiving the child abuse report from the Sex Offender Registry Board (SORB) when the SORB worker found that the sex offender was lying about his residence and living with children.

"And during your investigation, did you interview Mrs. Bartolli?" I picked up the investigation documents.

"Yes." Waters knew not to answer a question not yet asked.

"Please tell us about that conversation."

"The initial conversation or the later conversation?"

According to the investigation documents, Waters interviewed Mrs. Bartolli once, three days after the report came in. Lawyer shows stressed that a good attorney never asked a question if they didn't know the answer. I broke that rule on a regular basis and asked about criminal records, mental health admissions, and sex offender status. If the parent denied it, nothing lost, but often they elaborated on a history that the social worker knew nothing about. But having the social worker withhold information worried me. Nothing I could do about it; if I didn't ask now, the mother's attorney would ask later.

"You had two conversations with mother?"

"Yes, one during my investigation and one in the hallway this morning."

Strange that Waters neglected to tell me about the recent conversation. But it must be important if he now mentioned it. I'd take the conversations in order.

Asked him about the first conversation, the one in the documents. Mrs. Bartolli denied that she knew about the sex offender charges and stated that her boyfriend had never abused the children, or even yelled at them. I got the investigation documents entered into evidence.

"And you had a second conversation with Mrs. Bartolli today?" I picked up my yellow pad to take notes.

"Yes, in the hallway this morning."

"And that conversation is not in your investigation, now entered in evidence?"

"No, I just finished talking to her. I haven't had time to write it up."

"Please tell us about that conversation."

"Objection, that conversation was not included in the report."

"Your Honor." Both Attorney Wagner and I knew the objection was to give the other attorney time to regroup. "It is the admission of a party."

"Overruled. Answer the question, Mr. Waters."

"Mrs. Bartolli was upset about the children being removed from her home."

"Objection." Attorney Wagner, for Mrs. Bartolli, was on his feet. "Mr. Waters cannot know how my client felt."

"Sustained."

Waters knew better than that. I felt a chill up my spine; something didn't feel right. "Please tell us about what Mrs. Bartolli said."

"She said that her children missed her, and she wanted them back. Then she said that they may be better off in foster care, because her boyfriend hit them and left marks."

"I said no such thing," Mrs. Bartolli screamed. "He's lying." And she burst into tears.

I reached for the box of tissues, always kept in plain sight in Juvenile Court. I turned to hand them to Mrs. Bartolli.

Mrs. Bartolli struck the box of tissues to the floor. "I don't want nothing from the lying DCF. I just want my kids back."

Waters showed no reaction to the outburst. "Shall I continue with my testimony?"

Judge Hartwell looked over her half-moon glasses. "We will take a short recess to allow Mrs. Bartolli to compose herself. Recess for ten minutes."

Waters sauntered out of the courtroom. I followed at his heels. Waters headed for the stairs.

I placed myself in front of him, keeping my voice low. "Where are you going?"

"Going to have a cigarette." Waters took the pack from his pocket. "Is there a problem?"

"I need to talk to you. In a conference room." I watched Waters shake a cigarette from the pack and shrug. "Now. The cigarette can wait."

Waters followed me into the conference room. "What's the problem?"

"You know the problem. Why didn't you tell me about the second conversation with Mrs. Bartolli?"

"It just happened today. You were busy before court and I thought I'd surprise you with an admission."

"I don't like surprises. And it sounds like you made the story up. I wasn't that busy before court."

Waters carefully put the cigarette back into the pack and the pack back into his pocket. "Guess I'm not going to get to that right away."

I waited.

"I didn't make up the story. It's what she said." Waters maintained eye contact.

"You know it sounds suspicious. She denies and denies, we file, and the stakes go up and then she makes a hurtful admission. It doesn't make sense."

"If people were logical, we'd both be out of a job. I can't help it, it's what she said."

The court officer called the case back into the courtroom. The hearing took most of the day. At the end, Judge Hartwell gave custody to DCF, because of Mrs. Bartolli's admissions.

I was hungry and mad enough to spit nails. And I still had to go to the shooting club and deal with Troy. Protein first. The burrito truck was parked out front of the courthouse. Then I went to the bakery.

Meredith Shooting Club
Coke Kiln Road
Meredith, Massachusetts
6:00 PM

I was hyped up on sugar, pissed off at Waters and Troy, and now I was going to shoot a gun. Life just didn't get any better. Perseverance. I was going to continue the shooting course until I finished or was forced out. At least I remembered my old lady shoes and my shirt that buttoned to just below my chin. Looked sort of like the mother of the crazed shooter who talks about what a good boy her son was.

I pulled into the parking lot. Not as many people around today. Most stood around the door or on the porch of the main building. The storage shed stood open, its double doors revealing a mixture of metal targets, chairs, and a discarded desk.

Members of the class greeted me. Craig, seventeen years old with skinny arms and red hair, came over to sit down beside me. Mrs. Darrow was teaching the class this evening. Guess Troy was the teaching assistant. Once more, we went over gun safety and parts of the gun. Thank goodness it was review of stuff from Tuesday.

Mrs. Darrow droned on about ear protection and eye protection during the live fire. Range protocol and always be aware of your weapon and where it was pointed. Important stuff, but now I was really tired. At least it calmed me down.

The shooting range was in the basement of the club. A long room with concrete walls and windows high on the sides. Six shooting stations, each with a shelf and a clip for a target that could be placed up to fifty feet away. A shiny black gun was placed in front of me, with instructions not to touch it until told to do so.

Mrs. Darrow and Troy taught us how to stand and how to sight the gun. "Put your weight evenly on both feet. Let out a breath as you shoot." I didn't hit the target much, but the discipline of loading and shooting a weapon made me feel in charge.

Shooting a gun is fun.

"You're not hitting the target." Troy stood next to me and stated the obvious.

"I know. I'm not sure why."

"You're anticipating the firing of the bullet. You pull the weapon up at the end."

"I don't think so."

Troy picked up one of the brass casings from the floor. He passed it from one hand to another. Guess it was still hot. He put it on the barrel of my gun.

"If you're holding the weapon steady, the casing will stay on the barrel after you fire."

I stood on both feet, sighted the target, and fired. The casing rolled down the barrel and bounced off my shirt. At least I hadn't worn the low-cut number.

"Now practice firing until the casing stays in place." Troy went down the firing positions, giving advice to each person.

I tried to do as he advised. But when I was finished, there were a lot of casings on the floor. And not just from firing the gun.

"Class is over. Make your weapons safe." Mrs. Darrow clapped her hands as she said this. I knew that "make your weapon safe" meant removing the magazine and any bullets in the barrel and placing the magazine, the bullets, and the gun on the shelf of the shooting station.

Troy came over to collect my gun. "Why don't you collect the ear and eye protection and put it away?" he said. "We can meet upstairs after everyone has gone."

Meredith Shooting Club
Coke Kiln Road
Meredith, Massachusetts
8:42 PM

I put the eye protection and the colorful plastic ear muffs into the metal cabinet in the classroom. Craig, my red headed friend, tried to help but I waved him on. Mrs. Darrow and Troy were the last people up from the shooting range. She looked from me to Troy.

"It's okay, El. I have to talk to Niagara about something. I'll lock up."

"Be sure to check all three doors."

"We just checked the one downstairs."

Mrs. Darrow put her books into a bag and picked up her portable gun safe. "Check it again." She opened the door. "And don't forget the outside shed is still open. Guys were shooting pins earlier."

"Will do. I know the drill."

Mrs. Darrow left.

"Let's sit down." Troy gestured toward the classroom chairs.

"I'd rather stand."

"Okay. I want to tell you what happened."

"Maybe you should talk to your lawyer before you talk to me. I could use your admissions against you."

Troy ran his hand through his hair. "You going to be both prosecutor and witness?"

He had a point. I wasn't condemning anything. "I may not be the prosecutor for much longer. Conflict of interest. Then I could be a witness."

"I'll take that chance." He sat down. "I told you I hadn't seen my kids in a while. My ex-wife left me a few years ago. I was in the Army, a corporal, and she left me for a colonel. Around more and better pay. Didn't stay with him long but, next thing I knew, she and the kids were out of the country. Not on a military base, but somewhere in Peru, according to her sister. Brought them to see me about six months ago. Didn't even recognize Andrew and he didn't recognize me. Not sure if he's mine or the colonel's kid. But my daughter, Alexis, is crazy about her brother. Wish you'd sit down."

I folded my arms and leaned back against the metal cabinet. "I like it fine here. Why do you call her Alexis? I thought her name was Debbie."

"Margaret changed their names to make it harder to trace them. We've sort of agreed to call them Debbie and David because the kids are more comfortable with those names. But sometimes I still think of them by the other names.

"Anyway, Margaret, my ex, always drank a bit too much. Now it looks like she's got other problems too. I guess, shortly after I saw the kids six months ago, she left them with the Halls. Changed their names to Debbie and David, got some forged papers, I'm not clear on the details. Never even thought to call me to take the kids."

I didn't want to hear this. I started to pick up my papers and book.

"Don't you want to hear the rest of the story?"

"I'm not the one you should be talking to. You should talk to your lawyer or the judge, but not me."

"I just want you to know that I looked for my kids. I thought they were in Peru and I was going through the craziness of finding them there. Each province or state or political division in that country has its own rules and procedures. It was frustrating, but I didn't stop looking. I came to New England as soon as I found out she was here."

"I'm leaving now. I don't want to have this conversation. This is the kind of conversation you get in trouble for. As a lawyer, and a prosecutor, I should know better."

"Let me lock up and I'll walk out with you." Troy picked up the keys and went down the stairs.

I wasn't waiting for any more of his confessions. It was unprofessional and didn't do either of us any good. I stepped outside onto the porch. Three vehicles in the parking lot. My RAV4, Troy's pickup truck, and a nondescript sedan in some dark color, maybe black, navy, or dark green. Someone was sitting in the driver's seat. I could see the red glow of a cigarette. Maybe somebody waiting to talk to Troy. Good, that'd get the attention off me.

I started down the stone steps to the asphalt parking lot. The steps were covered with fallen leaves and I misjudged the step. Didn't fall, but I dropped my purse, my book, and my papers. The wind picked them up and scattered them across the parking lot. I ran after the papers.

The driver got out of the sedan and stood by the driver's door. I thought he meant to help me, but he continued to smoke his cigarette. I gathered up the papers and books and put everything back in my purse. I unlocked the car and piled everything on the front seat.

As I pulled out my keys, I remembered the shed. I hadn't made a promise to Troy, but I'd make sure everything was in there before I left.

A couple of shooting pins leaned against the outside. I picked them up and placed them inside the shed. It was darker in this section of the parking lot, so I flipped the switch to make sure I got everything.

A man stood inside the shed. Under the light, I recognized him as the man at the hospital wearing a Batman t-shirt. Only this time, instead of a knife, he was holding a gun.

"Sit down," he said, motioning to a wooden chair up against the wall.

"Sit down," he said again. "Or something worse will happen."

I sat.

"She don't want me back." He waved the gun. "Because of *you.*"

"I can help you with that," I said. "I can tell her that you won't be arrested and that DCF will help you get back together. What do you need me to do?" Now I was babbling.

Batman pulled both double doors until they closed and fitted a wide plank into the slots on either side, creating a barrier between us and the rest of the world.

I stood up and started toward the door.

"Don't do that." Batman pointed the gun at me.

I picked up one of the broken chairs and threw it at him. He ducked, and the chair splintered on the dirt floor behind him. While he was disoriented and not pointing the gun at me, I tried to run past him. I was almost at the door when he tackled me.

It hurt, but I managed to get a few inches closer to the door, even when we were on the ground. My shoulder hurt. I knew the worst position was face down on the ground, so I tried to roll over. The pain radiated around my neck. Still on the ground, but at least I could see Batman, who still had the gun. I kicked at him. Kicking someone in the groin is harder than it looks on television. But I did manage a decent kick to the shins.

Batman fell back against a rack of metal targets, knocking them over. It created a deafening sound in the small shed. He got back on his feet before I did and found his gun. I tried to stand, and he pushed me back down onto the dirt floor. I would have a bruise, if I lived long enough.

On my back, on the floor, I dug my fingers into the dirt, hoping to throw it in his face. A few stray rocks came up, but years of feet tramping in and out had packed it down hard. I felt a breeze and realized the door did not go to the floor. There was a gap of about three inches between the bottom of the door and the dirt floor. I grabbed the bottom of the door and pulled myself toward it. Rattled the door. It didn't move.

"You are more trouble than you are worth," said Batman. He raised the gun and pointed it at me.

The entire door shook when something hit the outside.

"Niagara!" It was Troy. "Niagara, open the door!"

"Your girlfriend is with me now," shouted Batman. "I didn't want to kill anyone, but you're making it hard not to. Step away from the door or I'll shoot her and then you."

No sound came from outside. I slid closer to the door, getting dust in my eyes and hair. Still trying to get enough dirt in my hands to throw at Batman.

He raised the gun again.

I tried to slide back toward the door. My foot slipped, and I sprawled on the dirt. I once again grabbed the door from my position on the ground and shook it. It didn't give way.

My hand was pulled under the door. Troy. At least I would have a connection to Troy, in my last few moments. His hand, warm and rough, comforted me.

Something cold and metallic replaced Troy's warm hand. I wanted his hand back and opened mine. His fingers closed around my hand, lodging the metallic object in the center. He pushed my hand back under the door.

I realized there was a gun in my hand seconds before it registered with Batman. But seconds were all I needed. The revolver fit snuggly in my hand. I pointed it upward. Batman started to bring up his weapon, larger and heavier than the one I held.

Targeting the center mass of his body, I fired the gun. I expected a recoil but didn't feel anything. I shot again. He went down.

Troy pounded on the door. "Niagara, open the door."

I waited for Batman to get up again. He stayed down. I pushed up from the floor, dusted myself off, and picked up Batman's gun and put it next to mine on a desk, out of his reach. With some difficulty, I lifted the plank holding the door closed. It slipped from my hands and fell to the ground. Working around it, I got the door open.

I didn't see Troy at first. He was still on the ground. I realized he must have been there to hand the revolver. He stood up and hugged me. At least we could both still stand.

It was cold, and I started to shiver. Troy checked Batman who moaned when Troy lifted him. Not taking any chances, Troy put him into a wooden chair and tied him with some rope he found in the shed.

"Both the chair and the rope are old, but I think it'll hold him until the police get here." He picked up both guns and moved them outside the shed.

Troy put his jacket around me.

"Where did you get the .38?" I asked.

"It's a gun club, darling," he said.

I shivered again. Don't know whether it was the cold or the darling. Troy wrapped his arms around me and we sat on the ground until the red and blue flashing lights came into the parking lot.

I shot a man. More than once.

FRIDAY, NOVEMBER 5

Logan Community Hospital
100 Amanda Street
Meredith, Massachusetts
6:38 AM

I woke in a strange place. White walls and white bed and a huge clock with huge numbers and a second hand on the wall. A hospital. I was in a hospital. Still had my clothes on but they were covered with dirt and blood.

Troy. And the man with the Batman t-shirt. Who now had a real name, but I couldn't remember it. Ambulances and police officers at the shooting club. A trip to Logan Hospital, as it was the closest place with an emergency room. Batman, his real name was Gary LaValley, needed to be life flighted by helicopter to Worcester. Couldn't get up much sympathy for him.

My wounds were not serious. I stayed at Logan Hospital in Meredith after LaValley went by helicopter to the Worcester hospital. I was comforted by the thought that LaValley and I weren't in the same hospital.

Troy. I needed to find Troy. I rolled out of the bed and stepped out of the cubicle into the chaos of the emergency room.

"Miss, can I help you?" said a voice.

I looked down into the brown face of Dr. Rehan. He looked like he may have been working since the last time I'd seen him, almost a week ago.

"Fontaine. Niagara Fontaine. We met last week."

His face registered nothing.

"I need to know about Troy Higgins. He came in with me tonight."

"He's down the hall," said Dr. Rehan. "You should see him soon."

"Is he okay? He wasn't hurt, was he?"

"Just some bruises and a huge splinter." Rehan said. "I can't tell you much else."

Dr. Rehan guided me back into the room I had just left. I still had all my clothes on but wanted to climb in bed anyway. A state police officer entered the room. Nice boots and silver buttons. Dr.

Rehan nodded and left.

"I need to ask you a few questions," he said, taking out a device. Unlike me, he seemed to prefer digital note taking. "I'm Trooper Barry."

"Niagara Fontaine," I said. "But you know that."

Adrenaline will only take you so far. "But I am exhausted right now and need to find Troy Higgins."

"Mr. Higgins is fine. He tells me this isn't the first time you had problems with Mr. LaValley." Trooper Barry took out a notebook. "Funny nothing about your previous encounter showed up in the police records."

I sat back down. "I was in a hurry that night."

"Too much of a hurry to report an armed assailant?"

"I was going to the scene of Scarlett Scarletti's murder. The teenager allegedly killed by her father?"

"I know the case," said Trooper Barry. "Spoke to Alvarez about it."

Couldn't tell if he thought that was good or bad, so I said nothing. I went through the events of last night and he asked me questions.

"I could arrest you, you know." Trooper Barry slid his notebook back into his pocket. "For assault with a deadly weapon, at least."

"Are you going to arrest me?"

"Not right now. You're not a flight risk. Don't even have a passport. But don't leave the area or I might change my mind."

"You've been checking on me." I stood up again. "Can I go now?"

"No." He gestured at my shirt. "We're going to need your clothes for forensics. Do you need a nurse to help you undress?"

"No, I can manage it myself."

"Put one piece of clothing in each paper bag." He pointed to a stack of bags on the floor that I hadn't noticed before. "Put on the scrubs they left for you."

After he left, I took off my clothes, including my underwear. One piece in each bag. Put on the scrubs. Felt half dressed in no underwear and only the polyester scrubs between me and the outside world.

Trooper Barry came back into the room and started collecting and sealing bags. I walked out, and Trooper Barry didn't stop me.

Troy was standing in the hallway. His arm was bandaged.

"Niagara, let's go home," he said. "I don't know about you, but I need to sleep."

"How are you doing? Did you get hurt?"

"Yeah, I've been released. Nothing serious, I drew some blood pounding on the door. Doc had to remove a splinter or two." He looked me up and down. "Interesting outfit."

I looked down. The scrubs hid very little.

"But I'm too tired to care. Adrenaline is wearing off fast." Troy put his arm around my waist and we walked out of the hospital.

He took me home, but I don't remember much of the ride. Troy followed me into my apartment and into my bedroom.

"Thought you might need these too," said Troy. He held up my purse and my papers from class.

"How did you get those?" I took them from him and put them on the nightstand. "Never mind, I don't care."

I climbed into bed with the scrubs still on. At least they were clean. Troy continued to stand by my bed.

"Thanks for bringing me home. I appreciate it."

"I'm not leaving you. I'll sleep on the couch." He headed for the door.

"The couch is five feet long and scratchy," I said. "I'm practically asleep anyway. We can share my bed."

I heard him take off his shoes. I don't remember anything after that.

Troy was gone when I woke up. Propped up next to my purse was a note: "Called DCF and said you would be late today. Call them if you take the day off. Made coffee. Call me if you want company. Troy"

I didn't want to talk to anybody just now. I poured a cup of coffee and sat at the kitchen table going over the events of the night before. LaValley tried to shoot me, so I shot him. I felt bad about it last night but, in the daylight, I couldn't work up much sympathy for what he did. If he died, I might feel worse.

Looking out the window, I saw TV vans and reporters in the parking lot. Mrs. Schmidt was talking to someone from Channel 4, the Boston station.

I heard a knock on my door.

"Who is it?" I asked. Alvarez would approve.

"Ben Case. WWLP News. I have a few questions."

How the hell did he get in here? I was glad I didn't open the door. "No comment!" I yelled.

"I would like to hear your version of the shooting," he persisted.

"No comment."

I went into the bedroom to get ready for work. They had security there.

Department of Children and Families
Legal Division
45 Maple Street
Worcester, MA
11:05 AM

The summons came shortly after I arrived at the office, nonchalantly dropped on my desk by a clerk in a straight skirt and high heels. As the clerk tap-tapped away, I wondered why I had never seen this woman in the office before. The dazzling white envelope lay on my desk, cold and anticipatory.

I slit open the stiff envelope.

"A complaint has been filed against you for conduct as an employee of the Commonwealth of Massachusetts. Specifically, the complaint alleges commission of an assault and a conflict of interest. Please plan to appear in my office on Friday, November 12 for a review of these charges. It is suggested that you bring your union representative with you at that time."

Commission of an assault. I shot a man. Wounded him. Still waiting to see if I'd be charged. And, because this was a government job, conflict of interest was included. That was my involvement with Troy. Did I want to be involved with the father of children in foster care? Did he want me to be involved, other than to help him get the children back? The envelope, once so crisp, was crushed and soggy in my hand.

Jacque walked into my office without knocking. "Bad news?" He gestured to the envelope.

"You mean other than the fact that I shot a man? With a gun that wasn't mine?" I put the envelope on the desk and ran my hand over it, trying to flatten it again. It didn't help. "And conflict of interest. They know about me and Troy."

"That was fast. Thought you only shared your secrets with me."

I stared at Jacque. It was fast. How did the General Counsel learn about me and Troy? I didn't tell him. Unlikely that Troy did.

"I didn't think of that." I picked up the envelope again. "How did the info get to McMasters and up the chain of command? I only learned about the conflict less than eighteen hours ago."

"Makes you wonder." Jacque pulled a bag of gummy bears out of his pocket. "Want one?" He knows I hate gummy bears.

"You know something."

"Not much but, yeah, something. Was at a local dive last night. Waters, your favorite social worker, was there, talking about how you were in trouble again. With another cop. How he tried to save you."

"Save me?"

"That's his story." Jacque popped another gummy bear into his mouth.

"Why, he...he..." I banged my hand on the desk. "I'd say what I think of him, but I'm a lady."

Jacque smiled. "You ain't no lady. You just can't think of a word bad enough for him. A lawyer without words is a scary thing."

Leave it to Jacque to point out the absurdity in any situation. I took a deep breath.

Barbara pounced on us as soon as we left the conference room. "Attorney Fontaine, you're wanted on the phone."

"Take a message."

The receptionist was insistent. "You're the only attorney here and Kara said that it was an emergency."

I said goodbye to Jacque and went back into my office to answer the phone.

"Niagara, Anna Miller has shown up. She's in my office." Kara Salem sounded like she was out of breath.

Anna Miller. I tried to place the name. Oh, yes, the Miller children sent home by Judge Hartwell. The Miller children who were not in DCF custody. Not sure, but I think Anna was the oldest.

"Why is the child with you?" I asked. "We don't have custody of her."

"Anna came to me. Said her mother took off with the boys. Left her alone at the house. She's been staying on and off with a neighbor over the last week. The neighbor can't keep her, so she brought her here."

"What does she mean, her mother 'took off'? Why didn't she go with her?"

"Anna said that a man named George came to the house and her mother left with him. He didn't want Anna to go."

"And there isn't anybody to take care of her?"

"No. We don't know who her father is, and the neighbor can't keep her. I can find a foster home for her tonight, but I'll have to file tomorrow."

I took notes automatically. "Write the affidavit, outline the situation, and ask for custody. Email it to me when you're finished."

Kara was silent for thirty seconds. "Can we go after mom and the twins?"

"We don't know where they are. And the twins aren't going to tell."

"Nine months old, I guess not. I'll fax the affidavit when it's finished."

I hung up the phone.

It rang again almost immediately. Kara Salem again.

"Anna is freaking out." Kara started the conversation without a greeting. "I'm taking her to the hospital to be psychiatrically screened. She says she's going to kill herself."

"What do you want me to do?"

"Just wanted to let you know that you won't get an affidavit today. I'm taking presumptive custody, going with Anna to the hospital, and I'll file on Monday."

My cell phone rang. "I need to get this."

Jacque sounded out of breath. "Margaret Lindstrom has disappeared with her children. Debbie and David Hall, the kids we picked up the night Scarlett died."

As if I needed a reminder. "What do you mean disappeared? Is this an epidemic?"

"An epidemic? Who else disappeared?"

"Never mind, Jacque. Where did they go? Do we have any leads?"

"We're tracking down all known relatives now. I'll let you know if anything works out."

"Thanks. Keep me informed."

"And there's news about LaValley, the guy you shot."

As if I could forget who LaValley was.

"What news?"

He's going to make it. But he's making noises about suing you for shooting him."

"Suing me?"

"Just running off his mouth. Right now, we need to get more information about the missing kids.

I went into the reception area.

Troy stood there, his face colorless. "My children are gone. Again."

SATURDAY, NOVEMBER 6

Troy and I were in Brattleboro, Vermont. I was suspended from my job, so there was no reason to stay around the office. And Troy couldn't work and was going stir crazy. We followed the only lead Troy had. About eight weeks ago, Margaret had been in touch with her sisters, Marlene and Mary, who lived in Brattleboro. After Mary told Troy about the visit, he came to New England. Maybe Mary could help us find the children again.

As interstate highways go, Route 91 was one of the more pleasant ones. I had been on most sections of the road from Hartford almost to Canada. It ran through farmland and small cities. The stretch from Greenfield, Massachusetts to Brattleboro, Vermont was wooded and drew leaf peepers in the fall. Now, in November, the trees were bare, and the wind whipped across the highway.

"Tell me about Margaret and her sisters," I said.

"What do you want to know?"

"Well, you're dragging me to Vermont to see them. That must mean something."

"Margaret and her sisters, Marlene and Mary, are all Army brats. Followed their father around to Army bases, always trying to make new friends and fit in. Mary, the oldest, took care of everyone. Marlene, the youngest, expected everyone to take care of her. Margaret was stuck in the middle."

"How did you meet Margaret?"

"At Fort Benning in Georgia. I was eighteen and Margaret was fifteen when we met. I had just joined the Army, she was living with her parents on base. A few moves later, she and her parents were ordered to the base where I was stationed. She was eighteen by then. We'd known each other for three years but spent most of it apart. Thought we were in love."

We passed through Brattleboro, past the Lachis Hotel and went north on Route 5 to Marlene's address of the "State Road 6, Lot 4" variety. Troy said it was a trailer park. Rural Vermont never bought into the necessity of zoning. Rows of hot metal cubes, ringed by rusting cars and discarded toys, dotted the land. Arising behind these acres of squalor were the Green Mountains, the stark beauty mocking the tiny people below.

"So how did they get to Vermont?" Georgia to Vermont was a leap.

"After Andrew was born, Margaret had a hard time. Blamed it all on me. Left me for a colonel. Guess he was more like her father than I was. Though daddy issues weren't Margaret's main problem."

"I think we turn here," I said. "Sign says Green Acres Estates are this way."

The road got narrower and the potholes more frequent.

Troy continued his story. "Margaret drank. She didn't think I noticed, but I'd find the empty bottles. Didn't want to leave her alone with the kids, so I invited Mary to stay with us. She left shortly after Mary showed up."

"When was this? Have you seen her since she left?"

"Just over a year ago. I tried to look for her, even found the colonel. Army keeps good records. But by the time I found him, she had left the U.S. and was living in Peru."

"Peru?" I was surprised. "Why Peru?"

"Damn if I know. She stayed there for about seven months. Peru keeps lousy records, so I couldn't locate her. Few months ago, Mary contacts me to say she heard her sister was in Vermont. Or the Berkshires. So, I came up here to find her. Then she disappeared again."

Troy turned into the driveway marked "Green Acre Estates. Fine Prefabricated Homes." Just inside the gate, four teenage boys in baggy jeans and bandanas stood in the middle of the road. Wannabe gangstas, even in Vermont. The boys stared at us.

Troy beeped the horn. Urban gangs and urban violence were unlikely here.

The boys ambled to the side of the road, kicking up gravel on the way.

We pulled up to the tiers of mailboxes in the entryway. Stuck on letters. Number thirteen. The letters were crooked, with the two LLs in Miller riding above the rest of the name. Lot 13. Maybe our lucky number.

It took some looking, but we found the fine prefabricated home with a 13 out front. The trailer had a water stain, brown and shaped like the state of Michigan. Sections of the skirting fell away, exposing the wheels.

Two children played with the filthy toys scattered across the brown lawn.

"That's Timothy and Thomas, Marlene's four-year-old twins," said Troy. "Timmy, the dark-haired one, looks like Marlene. Don't know who Tommy looks like."

Timmy spotted us first. "Unca Troy. What you doin' here?"

We got out of the car. "Hi, guys. Is your mother home?"

The screen door slammed. "She ain't here." A woman appeared, wearing shorts despite the autumn chill. She wiped her hands on a towel.

Troy did his best to smile. "Hi, Marlene. How are you and the boys?"

She threw the towel over her shoulder. "She ain't here. I ain't seen my sister for months." Marlene ignored me.

"Was she here a few months ago? Why didn't you call me?"

"Don't want to get in the middle. Besides, she's only here to borrow money. I said no, she left."

By this time, both children hung onto Troy's clothing.

"Unca Troy, can you take us to the creek?" Timmy pulled on Troy's pant leg. "Mom says we need a 'dult."

Troy looked at Marlene.

"Go ahead, take them," she said. "Ain't going to give me no peace until you do."

"So, Unca Troy, where Auntie 'Ret?" Timmy pulled Troy along, before his mother changed her mind.

"I haven't seen Auntie Margaret much lately." Troy turned to me. "This is my friend Niagara."

"That's a funny name." This from Tommy.

Timmy interrupted. "That's not a nice thing to say."

"It's okay," I said. "Where are we going?"

"To the pond. To catch frogs. I'm sorry."

I think the last was Tommy's apology, not anything to do with the pond or the frogs.

Troy picked up a rock. "So, have you seen Aunt Margaret?"

"Mom says it's secret," said Timmy.

"Not supposed to tell," said Tommy.

"I won't tell anybody. Promise."

Tommy stopped talking but Timmy continued to give information. "Yeah, she here. She bot us gum and pops. She did supper and slept on the couch. Mommy and her were nice in the beginning."

"At the beginning?"

"Yeah, when she got here. She played with us and brought us DS2s. I can play Mario Brothers on it. Want to see?"

Tommy interrupted. "I want to go to the pond."

"And we will. Let's go. Maybe we'll do the DS thing another day."

The boys brought a battered net with them. They caught two frogs and were soaked to the knees. It was barely 50 degrees, but the boys didn't seem to mind.

"You said Mommy and Aunt Ret were nice at the beginning," said Troy. "Then what happened?"

"Then, in the morning, they yelled and Ret left." Timmy was studying a dragonfly that landed on a log. It moved erratically; probably too cold for it to buzz around.

"What were Mommy and Margaret yelling about?"

"Bout 'dult stuff," said Tommy, crouching down to study an ant hill. "We go outside."

We caught two frogs and a dragonfly. Not bad for a day's work.

We dropped the boys back with Marlene, but she continued to ignore us. Next stop, looking for Mary.

We headed up 91 to Dummerston, the next small town off the highway. Mary's tiny ranch house sat at least a half mile from its nearest neighbor. In contrast to the trailer, the immaculate house sported mums and purple kale in the late season garden. Warm and inviting.

Troy hopped out of the car. I followed more slowly.

Mary met him on the porch. "Leave. Now."

"Mary, what's the problem? I'm not the enemy."

"Not you. That no-good sister of mine. Now leave." Mary looked around Troy. "Who did you bring with you?"

"A friend. Her name is Niagara."

Mary made no comment about my name or my being with Troy. "Has Margaret been here?"

Mary stared at Troy. "Like you don't know. She shows up a few months ago, stays here for a week, and all hell breaks loose when she leaves."

"She was here? Wait a minute. You called to tell me you thought Margaret was in Vermont, but you didn't say you actually saw her. Why didn't you call me?"

"She's my sister, and she asked me not to call you. So, I didn't. Thought my chatterbox sister Marlene'd tell you anyway."

Troy lowered his voice, so Mary had to lean forward to hear him. "What happened? Why are you upset with her?"

"What didn't happen? The state police come, and the child welfare people come, and I expect the Intergalactic Space Patrol at any minute. All asking questions about her and threatening me if I don't talk."

"And all these people were looking for Margaret?"

"That's what they said. Finally believed I didn't know anything and left."

"Why were they looking for her?"

Mary shrugged. "Damn if I know. They sure asked a lot of questions, though. Where she went, who she saw, who she called. Told them she sat on my couch for five days, watching TV. No visitors, no trips to the food store, no money for what she ate."

"C'mon Mary. I know you. You must've asked them questions."

"Yup. And they didn't give no answers. So I stopped talkin' to 'em." Mary opened the door to the house. "Like I'm goin' to stop talking to you now." She went back into the house.

Why were all these people looking for his ex-wife? And where were the children? Neither Marlene nor Mary had mentioned them.

Troy walked up the front steps and knocked on the door. It swung open at his knock. He turned to me and said, "Just like Mary, to leave with maximum drama and then not lock her door."

"Mary?" He peered into the gloom.

"What?"

"Where is Debbie? David? Were my kids with Margaret?"

"No. She said she left them with friends in Massachusetts. The child welfare people asked where they were too." Mary stopped in front of Troy. "Haven't seen the kids for some time. Don't seem like they're an important part of either her life or of the no-count colonel."

Mary walked by him and out the door. And turned around and came back in. "But some mail came for her after she left. Do you want it?"

"Yes."

"It may take me a few minutes to find it. Have a seat." She finally looked at me and acknowledged my existence. "You too. Can't offer you coffee or anything, I got to go to work soon."

Mary came back into the room with an envelope. "I got a Verizon bill. It's mine but it had some charges I didn't make.

"I put it all in this envelope. Was going to ask her for payment if she ever showed up with money. Like that's going to happen." She pulled several sheets of paper out of the envelope. "The phone calls marked in yellow are the ones she made."

Troy skimmed the bills quickly. "Where is Deer Lick, Vermont? She called there at least twenty times."

"There's nothing in Deer Lick, Vermont."

He stared at her. "But obviously you know the place. Why?"

"Marlene and Margaret and I went to summer camp there, a hundred years ago. The place may not even be standing."

"Maybe it is. What's the name of the camp?"

"Some combination of nature and religion. Wild Deer Camp of Christ or something. Mom sent us there in the summer. She often got religion in the summer. And it got us out of her hair."

We looked through the other receipts. She bought a shirt and nightgown at Walmart in New Hampshire and vitamins—Vitamin C, Vitamin B, and folic acid—at the local drug store.

"Can we take these with us?" I asked.

"Sure, it's not like she's ever going to pay me back."

Mary walked past us and to the door. "I got to go to work." She disappeared, and I heard a car start.

Troy looked after her. "Guess we get to lock the door."

Route 91
Bernardston, Massachusetts
6:45 PM

I looked out the window. The green forests and hills were giving way to billboards and warehouses. We were back in Massachusetts. Not sure we had learned anything.

"What's the plan from here?" I asked. "Did we learn anything useful?"

"Margaret seems to have been around for a few weeks. Must be some reason she came to New England." Troy passed a Volvo going 40 miles an hour on the interstate. "And she seems to have spent a lot of time talking to people in Deer Lick, Vermont. My plan is to go there and ask questions. Probably be there for a couple days and won't be coming back and forth to Massachusetts. Want to come with me?"

"I don't know. A day looking for your kids is one thing. But if you plan to stay in Vermont for a few days, I don't know. You're still the father of a kid in state custody. And I may still be facing criminal charges."

"Both those things are true. But you will be taken off my case, or you'll take yourself off the case and the conflict will be resolved. And there is nothing you can do about LaValley now. Except wait. Do you want to sit around and wait or do something while you are waiting?"

He had a point.

SUNDAY, NOVEMBER 7

Main Street
Deer Lick, Vermont
8:40 AM

When we stopped for breakfast in Deer Lick, Vermont, it was raining. When we got back to the car, it was raining harder. The world outside was dripping wet. Drippy trees, drippy eaves, drippy windshield. I fumbled with my umbrella, feeling a cascade of water run down my back.

"With a name like Niagara, I guess you like this kind of weather."

"My parents named me for their honeymoon place, not for my love of being cold and damp."

"We need to find my kids soon." Troy started the engine and welcome heat blew into my face. Whoosh. Water blew past all the car windows as Troy hit the puddle covering the entire entrance to the restaurant. We turned left toward the main street.

"I've got a plan for today. First, we go to the local police station and check with the desk officer. See if we can check the police log. Maybe Margaret needed money, or somebody remembers the kids. In a town of less than 5,000, a stranger may have been noticed. Then we can track down Lemore Dinsmore, that's the person Margaret called. If he exists. And we need a place to stay.

Troy was more talkative in Vermont. Yesterday, going on about Margaret and then his plans for today. Maybe he was anxious or apprehensive. Or maybe he just wanted to let me in on his plan.

Troy pulled into the police station parking lot. "Well, let's see what we can find out here."

I got out and walked around the car to Troy. Then tripped over the curb stone. He reached to keep me from falling. Maybe Troy wasn't the only one who was anxious and apprehensive. I didn't have a plan to share with him.

I righted myself and walked up the steps ahead of Troy.

The officer at the desk looked like every other desk cop in every other precinct in the country. Somewhere between thirty and forty, with a balding head, and wearing a standard issue uniform with military darts sown into the shirt. Except that he was reading a

Suzanne Brockman novel. And not hiding it. Things were different in Deer Lick.

"May I help you?" The desk officer's name plate said he was Officer Deidrick. He laid the book aside and looked up with a smile, as if he were genuinely trying to be helpful.

"I'm wondering if you could give me some information. I'm looking for a fugitive who may have two young children with her. Goes by the name of Margaret Lindstrom or Margaret Higgins." Troy did his best cop-to-cop voice, standing squarely on both feet, his right hand resting where his gun would be if he had one. He did everything but flip a badge at this guy.

"You a cop? Got a warrant of apprehension?"

Troy was in full cop-mode now. "No, just asking questions at this point. Need to know if anybody's seen her. Short, red haired woman with two blond kids. Maybe driving a rental car. May have dyed her hair though."

"A lady fugitive? With two kids? Why'd she bring her kids? That would only slow her down. I'd remember if I'd seen something like that."

I imagined a picture of Margaret with the word "Fugitive" tattooed across her forehead. I couldn't recognize a fugitive on sight and doubted if this officer could either.

"I'm just looking for anything unusual in your police log. A disturbance that turned out to be nothing when the police got there, reports of an unfamiliar woman with children."

"I can't let you go looking into the police log. It's confidential."

"It is very important that I find this fugitive. I won't copy anything. I'll only take notes. My associate here will help me." Troy gestured to me. Reduced to an associate without a name. "We won't be long."

"No, I can't let you look at the log. Had a forty-five-minute discussion last night at the select board meeting about not releasing information to the public. Not even addresses. In a town this small, people know who's doing what by where it happened."

"Nobody needs to know. It's just sharing information."

"Everybody'll know. The select board meetings are on local

access TV. Whole town can watch it if they're so inclined. People were complaining about being able to identify people from the logs. Nobody gets them." Officer Deidrick studied Troy, as if imagining a uniform on him. "What police agency did you say that you came from?"

Though I didn't practice municipal law, I was pretty sure the police logs were public records. Of course, we could make a formal request and wait for hours or days for a copy.

Troy looked at his watch, straightened his spine. "Can you review the logs over the last two weeks and let me know if you see anything unusual? A person familiar with this town ought to be able to pick out the strange things right away."

"I could do that. As you are from out of town, it's unlikely that you'd know anybody or that the addresses would mean anything to you." The officer shuffled through the logs for several minutes. Most of the daily logs were one page or less. On a particularly busy day, the log ran to two and a half pages.

"Only two things a little strange. Yesterday, Janie called from the diner to say that somebody left without paying. She didn't know who it was. On the same day, a lady called, and she'd broken down out on Highway 28. Told her that we weren't an auto club, but she was so upset that I sent Clem out with the wrecker. She wasn't there when he arrived. Other than that, we got local pickpockets and a few drunk arrests. And some kids jumping onto parked cars. Does that help you?"

"Yes, thanks, that's a good start. One more question. Do you know a man named Lemore Dinsmore?"

"Lemore Dinsmore. I thought you said you didn't know anybody in town."

"I don't. But Mr. Dinsmore may have some information that I need. Until now, I wasn't even sure that he existed."

"Oh, he exists all right." The officer returned the police log to its place on his desk. "Lemore's the one that goes on TV and complains about the logs being public. If he finds out I gave this stuff to you, I'll know where it came from and I'll come looking for you."

"He won't know. I just need to talk to him about some other

things. Where can I find him?"

The officer's eternally helpful nature come to the forefront again. "This time of day, he's probably down the street at his auto shop. Running Clem ragged, as usual."

"Is he open on Sunday?" I asked.

"Dinsmore does twenty-four-hour towing. And he's so tight with his money he'd stay open just in case somebody might come by for repairs. Probably got Clem there today too."

The tow truck pulled up in front of the gas station. Black smoke belched from the exhaust pipe. The body of the truck hadn't been washed since the Vietnam conflict. Neither Troy nor I spoke, primarily because we couldn't have been heard over the engine noise.

A blur of blue and red propelled itself from the driver's seat onto the ground.

"Dinsmore. Can I help you?"

I was impolite and stared. The man was five feet four inches on a good day, and almost as wide as he was tall. His head seemed to grow directly out of his shoulders without benefit of a neck and his biceps bulged so that he was forced to hold his hands at least a foot from his hips. I wondered how he unzipped his pants without lengthening his arms or contorting his entire body. This apparition had copper hair, a red and black buffalo check shirt, jeans, and red cowboy boots.

Troy recovered first. "Hello, Mr. Dinsmore. My name is Troy Higgins, and this is Niagara Fontaine. We'd like to talk to you."

"Talking appears to be what you're doing right now. And call me El—most everybody does. 'Cept for the ladies. They call me More, 'cause they always want more of me, know what I mean?"

Troy looked uncomfortable with Dinsmore's attempt at male bonding. "Mr. Dinsmore, I need some information. I'm looking for a woman."

"Lookin' for a woman, huh? Ain't we all." He turned to Niagara. "Looks like you got a good one here."

As if the thought of work had just struck him, Dinsmore walked over to the tow truck and started rummaging through the tool box attached to the side of the flat bed.

"Mr. Dinsmore." My turn to talk to him.

"Oh, yeah." He pulled a wrench, about a foot long, out of the box. "What do you need to know?"

I took a step back. He didn't look like he'd use it as a weapon, but you never know.

"About a woman, maybe with kids. A road service call yesterday."

"Didn't do the service calls yesterday. Clem did." Dinsmore walked over to a car with two feet sticking out the side. He kicked the soles of the feet. "Hey, Clem, come out here. We need to talk to you."

Clem, on a creeper with wheels, rolled out from under the car. I hadn't seen anybody crawl under a car in years. Thought it was all computerized these days.

Clem stood up. He was tall and thin, with his overalls, covered in grease and oil, hanging off him. His black hair stood out from under his cap and added to the unkempt look. "What you need to know?"

Dinsmore cut in. "Remember, yesterday, a service call? About 3 in the afternoon."

"Yeah. They weren't there when I got out there. Looked around for fifteen minutes. No car, no people. Took out the truck for nothing."

"And it costs me every time the truck goes out," Dinsmore said.

"That's it? Nothing else?" I really thought there should be more.

"Nope. Nobody there."

We turned to go. "Well, goodbye, El, Clem. Thanks." I felt I had to say something, as Clem was staring at me.

"Of course." Clem took off his hat, black around the inside rim, and scratched his head. "There is the other lady."

"What other lady?"

"The one I helped on the way back." Clem glanced at Dinsmore. "Helped her change her tire."

"You didn't call it in," said Dinsmore. "Didn't I tell you to always call it in when you do a road call?"

"Wasn't exactly a road call. She didn't have any money."

"So, now you're using my wrecker for charity. Ought to dock your pay for the time."

Clem passed his cap from one hand to the other.

"Clem, I'll reimburse you for your time." Troy held out a twenty-dollar bill. "What can you tell me about the lady?"

Dinsmore stepped up, as if to claim the money as his own. Troy slipped the bill into Clem's hand.

"Lady had two kids with her. Going to the conference center."

"Nobody goes to the conference center this time of year, Clem." Dinsmore tried to assert his authority. "You been smoking funny stuff again?"

"No." The cap made a few more turns in Clem's hands. "Thought she said she was going to the conference center. But it's closed. Didn't get a good look at her, I was changing the tire."

"Which way is the conference center?" I asked.

"North," said Clem, as if that explained everything.

"Did you notice anything else? What about the car?"

"2009 Chevy Impala. Rental car. Told her to call the rental company, but she said it was too far away. Kids were cute."

"Did she say anything else?" I had to be sure.

"Nope." Clem laid down and rolled back under the car.

Main Street
Deer Lick, Vermont
1:20 PM

We were no closer to answers than a week ago. An angry mother, a tow truck driver who fancied himself a stud, and lots of dead ends. Troy reached out and put his arm around my shoulders as we walked down the main street of town.

At least the town had decent food. We had gone back to the Main Street Diner for lunch. Macaroni and cheese. Classic comfort food.

After lunch, Troy didn't talk much. We just walked. Past the CVS pharmacy. We stopped in front of Abe's Hardware. A dusty display of Stanley screwdrivers and nails, sorted into plastic bins, adorned the front window. No chain store here. Abe probably decorated the window himself.

I saw a red and yellow reflection in the glass of the window. It moved quickly. Troy turned to get a better look. So did I.

The bright red and yellow parka kept moving. Its wearer was barely three feet high with long hair. A young girl, laughing and running into the street.

The driver in the Ford Silverado clanking down the street didn't see her. The pickup truck, with a plow attached early in the season, took up most of the street.

The young girl was headed right into the corner of the plow. The truck driver was probably on his phone as he was looking down.

I yelled "Stop!" He kept going.

Troy covered the width of the sidewalk in three strides. I thought the corner of the plow might take out his eye. He leaned over and grabbed the child by the back of the red and yellow parka and pulled her back with such force that he fell onto the sidewalk, the toddler in his lap. The plow passed just inches from her red shoes and Troy's boots. The driver never stopped.

The toddler started to scream. The adrenaline rush still lingered as I struggled to say something. Troy's breathing was fast, and his face was sweaty, despite the cold. I sat down on the curb next to where they'd fallen.

"Where did she come from?" I looked up and down the street, deserted now that the truck had moved on.

"What do we do now?" asked Troy.

The child made the decision for him. She got up and attempted to leave. He stood up in front of her and she kicked him. Troy knelt and put his hands on her shoulders, but she bit his fingers. He moved his hands away from her mouth and clamped them around her wrists. She continued to cry and struggled to get away.

I heard a door slam and steps came toward us from the hardware store.

"Let go of her." A short, dark haired woman stood there. She was Asian, maybe Filipino. Barely five feet tall, her round face sported wrinkles and a large, red mark on her neck. Though her pants had an L.L. Bean logo, they were two sizes too big and sagged around her ankles. The fleece jacket she wore pulled across her breasts.

The toddler escaped Troy's grasp and ran to the woman.

"Annie, I tell you no go in the street." As she spoke, the little woman ran her hands over the child's head, arms, and legs. "No bruises."

The child reached out to the woman and fell into her arms.

Who was this woman? They didn't look like mother and daughter. I doubted that anyone who lived in this town all year could afford a nanny. Maybe a baby-sitter.

"Momma." The girl spoke for the first time. "Home."

I felt my prejudices kick in. Everyone had them, but I needed to recognize and move past them. Vermont was the most Caucasian state in the U.S. Above 98%, if I remembered correctly. She could be the child's mother, though there was no physical resemblance. But in an isolated Vermont town, she was an anomaly. Anomalies bothered me.

"You're her mother?" Nothing like the direct approach.

"Yes." The woman looked directly at me. "Father is Navy seaman."

"Where do you live?" I realized I sounded like an interrogator. "Maybe we could give you a ride home."

"Outside town," said the woman.

Almost at the same time, the child said "camp" and offered me a sheet of paper. I took it.

The paper read, "My name is Clarissa. If I am lost, please return me to Camp Good News, 75 County Road, Deer Lick, Vermont." A phone number, in bold print, was circled in red.

"Clarissa? I thought you said her name was Annie," I said.

"You live at the camp?" Troy asked.

"She took the wrong paper." The woman took the paper from me, folded it, and put it in her pocket. "We go now."

"Do you live at the camp?" Troy repeated.

"Just in summer. We go." The woman took the toddler by the hand and set off down the street.

I put my hand on Troy's shoulder. "She could have said thank you."

"Or she could have explained why she called the girl Annie when the paper said Clarissa."

"Could be as simple as the kid took another girl's paper." I stared into the street. "But the child is a toddler. A little young for camp. Story doesn't hang together."

"Some religious camps, the whole family goes." Troy looked toward the hardware store. "She came out of there. Let's go ask some questions."

Troy held the door for me as we entered. Seems that Clem was not the only person who worked on Sunday. The store was narrow—maybe sixteen feet wide—but went deep into the building. Cardboard boxes were stacked against the right wall, all labeled in black marker. No apparent order to the boxes—3/8-inch hex bolts next to .22 rim fire ammunition.

On the left was a Plexiglas-enclosed counter. More cardboard boxes stacked on the top, these without labels. Handguns and knives were displayed in the cabinet.

At the far end of the counter sat three men in wooden chairs. Two had lit cigarettes and all three stared at us when we entered. Blue smoke filled the air.

The largest man, wearing a denim shirt, stood up. "Can I get you something?"

"Like to buy some ammunition," Troy said before I could open my mouth.

"Can't sell to non-Vermont people." Denim scratched his head.

"How do you know I'm not from Vermont?" One of the seated men snorted. "You ain't from around here."

Troy turned back to the large man. "The woman that just left, she buy ammunition?"

"No. And she never asked for it."

"Would you sell it to her?"

"She got a Vermont license, she lives in town. I can sell to her. But she didn't ask."

So she did live around here. These men didn't seem to be buying anything, so they may be here just to talk.

"She live up at the campground?" I asked.

"Not exactly a campground." The oldest of the men ground out his cigarette. "It's got cottages and buildings. Wood heat, not much insulation. They're summer homes."

"Are people living there now?" I asked.

"Not much longer," said the large man. "They all go somewhere else for the winter."

"Know where?" Troy pressed on.

"No." The large man came forward and put his hands on the counter. "You want to buy something?"

"Just looking."

I went through the boxes on the opposite wall. Lots of boxes but nothing that didn't belong in a hardware/general store that sold guns. Wrenches, bolts, hooks, and other unidentifiable metal objects. The large man followed all my movements.

"Looking for something special?"

"No. Noticed the last customer didn't buy anything either."

"She orders stuff."

"What kind of stuff?" I asked.

"Cribs. Baby bottles. Vitamins. Pole diggers. All kinds of stuff." The clerk turned to Troy. "You want any of that?"

"No, thanks." Troy took my arm and we left.

We walked back toward his truck. The street was still deserted.

"Well, at least we learned people are living at the camp." Troy stopped at the intersection, though nothing was moving.

"We learned more than that," I replied.

"What did you find out?"

"All those boxes along the wall were marked. Ones in front said what was in the box. Ones in the back had names on them."

"What names?"

"I assume the people that ordered them. Cookware, blankets, sheets, all with names and the address of the Camp Good News."

"Why'd they need all that stuff if they're going to go away soon?" Troy turned to me. "Good work."

We crossed the street.

"But it gets better," I said. "I didn't recognize most of the names on the boxes. But I did recognize one of them."

"Which one?"

"Amanda Simmons. She's Mr. Ames' assistant."

"Who's Mr. Ames?"

"You know, the dry-cleaning guy who does all the adoption commercials."

"Why would his assistant be getting deliveries in Vermont?"

"My question exactly. Maybe another Amanda Simmons."

We reached the truck. Troy opened the door. "I think we should explore this further. Are you coming?"

"What are you going to do? Just walk in there and ask them?" That didn't seem like a good idea to me. "How about a plan? Let's talk about this."

"We'll talk in the truck."

"Good," I said. "Because I've got a few ideas."

Somewhere on Old Turnpike Road
Deer Lick, Vermont
2:25 PM

Troy hadn't even argued when I suggested that we go out to Camp Good News to see who was staying there. Now in his truck, we were trying to get to the camp. No cell reception and no GPS in this section of Vermont.

We were stopped beside County Road. Had a paper map and GPS but neither were helping.

"No assault like a direct one." Troy studied a map of the conference center. "How about we go up to the front door and knock on it?"

"This is all your fine investigative skills can come up with?" I was cold and cranky. "Go in and knock?"

"Hey, if it doesn't work, I'll use my skills to come up with another plan. You got something better in mind?"

"No."

"Okay, then knock it is." He started the truck.

I scanned both sides of the only road in. On one side was a lake, probably used for swimming and canoeing when the camp was open. On the other side, many large buildings, most painted white, with some smaller individual dwellings in between. One directional sign pointed to the office, and dormitories, and activity center.

We followed the signs to the office. Unlike the other buildings, this one was sided in shingles left to weather to a dull gray. The building sprawled in several directions, as if added onto over the years by a series of uncaring carpenters.

We pushed open the unlocked door and entered a room lined with industrial plastic chairs.

"Looks like the principal's office," I said.

We looked around. Rows of chairs, many with graffiti on them, lined the room. There were clipboards in plastic slots next to a window that slid open. The outdated copies of "Parenting Today" and "Mommy and Me." Probably not standard reading for high school. I flipped through the magazines and pulled out the clipboards.

The form attached asked for name, identifying information, family composition, and a short medical history. No hint about what they did with the information.

Nobody was behind the sliding window. During the several minutes we looked around, nobody came in or out of the room. Maybe the place was deserted on Sunday.

Troy walked back into the hallway and proceeded away from the door. I followed. The room was a good-sized bathroom, with real cloth towels and facecloths. The corridor turned sharply to the right. The floor under my feet dropped away. Careless carpentry, or maybe the building settled unevenly over the years. Either way, I needed to step carefully.

Three doors on each side lined the corridor. The first door on the left was open. A conference room with a chart of each of the buildings, internal rooms drawn in and names applied. On the side was a whiteboard with an eraser. Looked like the names changed frequently. No Margaret Lindstrom or Hall or Higgins or any children with those names.

In the middle room, we found filing cabinets on three of the four walls. Troy tried the drawers, but they were all locked.

The third room contained a table that left no room for anything but two chairs. On the table was a computer.

I sat at the computer and thumped on the keyboard for a few minutes. "It's password protected."

"It figures. Let's just skip that for now."

We went back out into the hall. Standing in the hall, arms folded, was a tall, athletic woman. Sturdily built but well over forty. She had her hands folded over her nonexistent breasts.

"What are you doing here?"

I recovered before Troy did. "We're looking into the camp for our vacation next year. We were surprised you were open but couldn't find anybody."

"What are you doing here? You're not from around here," she repeated, as if I hadn't spoken.

"No, we came from Massachusetts. To look around."

"Nobody looks around here. No foliage, no sightseeing. I'm

calling the director. He'll deal with you." She gestured with an enormous hand. "Down here." We walked down the corridor and back into the waiting room.

"Wait here," she commanded. She walked behind the desk and picked up the phone. She dialed a few numbers and started gesturing. She turned her back on us.

Troy signaled to me and we left the building.

"Now what?" I hopped into the truck.

I was surprised nobody followed us out of the building. Troy looked around. The Amazon seemed to be the only person here.

"We'll come back after dark," he said.

"That's only in a few hours," I said.

"Not tonight," said Troy. "We need more information first."

"About what?"

"Who owns the camp? What do they use it for? Property this size must have records of ownership, tax records, and other paper. Some of it we can get online."

"And I know just the person to help us," I said.

It was Sunday night in Vermont. If we wanted to review paper records, we needed to wait until the town and state offices were open on Monday. We hopped in the truck and headed back to the motel.

MONDAY, NOVEMBER 8

Essex Hotel
Essex, Vermont
6:45 AM

I woke to darkness and, for a moment, didn't know where I was. The room, or what I could see of it by the light coming through the single window, was unfamiliar. Where's my backpack? I always took it to a new home. Pictures of Richard and my parents, a change of underwear, and food. Even then I needed food.

As my mental fog cleared, so did my recollection of yesterday's events. I was in Vermont. The harsh light coming through the window flashed "Motel—Vacancy." The room did look much like a foster home—bed, nightstand, desk and chair that could have been purchased from any discount furniture store. Just one bed, though. I didn't have to share this room with another child. Troy, next door, occupied his own room.

I smiled at the thought of sharing a room with Troy. Not just sex, though I might not object, but being with a genuinely nice guy. One who cared about his kids and was willing to go all out to find and protect them. But my second strongest trait was practicality, so that wasn't going to happen.

Yet, yesterday, he went out of his way to protect a child he didn't even know. And later, watching him in the hardware/general store. He'd done a good job, not that I was going to let him take the lead every time.

The room phone rang. I picked up the receiver.

"Niagara Fontaine." Even in the wilds of Vermont, my professional voice automatically answered the phone.

"Ready to go?" asked Troy.

"What's the plan for today?" I asked. "Though I just woke up."

"I'll meet you in about forty-five minutes. We can go to the Hall of Records or Registry of Deeds or wherever to find out who owns the conference center. Then go out and look around."

I noted the many uses of we and appreciated it. "See you in forty-five."

Took a quick shower, did my hair, put on minimal makeup and

was ready to go forty minutes later. No Troy.

Well, I might as well be useful. I dug the extra set of keys to Troy's truck out of my bag and opened the motel room door.

The temperature had dropped twenty degrees overnight. The wind blew dead leaves across the parking lot. Against stark outlines of the gray buildings glared across the parking lot. Frost accumulated on the windshield and on the parking lot.

Clad only in my jeans and denim jacket, I slid behind the wheel and started the truck, blowing on my frozen fingers.

A loud, flat sound made me jump. Troy's hand pounded on the window. I opened the passenger door and he slid in.

"What are you doing out here?" Troy's words came in white puffs as his breath hit the cold air.

"Starting the truck." As if that wasn't obvious. "I like being practical."

Troy held up his key ring, with a black plastic disk attached. "Do you know what this is?"

"No." I looked down at my key ring. "The key you gave me doesn't have one of those."

"That's because we only need one remote starter." Troy climbed in the truck.

"Remote starter?"

"Remote starter." Troy smiled. "So, you can get the truck started and stay inside where it's warm."

"Why didn't you tell me?"

"I would have. But you were so anxious to start you got here first." Troy settled back in the seat. "Or were you anxious to see me?"

"For that trick, you get to drive."

The search at the Registry of Deeds produced mixed results. The conference center had been owned by the Twelve Apostles Church in the 1940's and transferred to a series of corporations since that time. The latest transfer, and current owner, was a Massachusetts corporation going by the uninteresting name of the Deer Lick Conference Center. That transfer was in 2002.

Troy wanted to go immediately to the conference center to look around.

"I think we need some more information." I re-shelved the heavy Registry of Deeds books. Only the last five years of transfers were digitalized.

"What else do we need to know?"

"The Amanda Simmons thing still bothers me. What does she, or Ames Dry Cleaning, have to do with the conference center? Is it the same Amanda Simmons?"

Troy put the last book back. "What do you want to do?"

"There's a library in town with computers. Probably quicker than service in the motel."

I remembered Troy's frustration the night before. The motel advertised Internet access but in Deer Lick that meant slow, antiquated service.

"And they may have local papers with more information," Troy added. "Let's go."

The Massachusetts corporation that bought the center in 2002 had the statutory minimum of three officers—Sterling White, William Anders, and Amanda Simmons. Amanda Simmons seemed to be all over this, but in what capacity? Neither Troy nor I recognized the other two names, and nothing came up when we Googled them. The local weekly paper, the Deer Lick Gazette, made no mention of the transfer or the conference center in 2002 or since.

When we finished, it was almost four and the sun was setting.

After some argument, I persuaded Troy to leave the visit to the conference center for a later day.

We picked up sandwiches at a Gibson's Market as there was no McDonald's in Deer Lick and went back to the hotel room.

In Troy's room, every surface was covered by books and papers and his laptop was open on the only desk in the room. I spread a towel on the floor and we ate there. I placed a candle on the top of the television.

"Where'd you get the candle?" Troy bit into his ham sandwich.

"I bought it at the store with the sandwiches." I struck a match and lit the candle. "Thought it'd smell better than this room. Do you like sandalwood?"

"Sandalwood is fine." Troy took another bite.

"Is this considered glamorous investigation work?" I unwrapped my tuna with cheese. "Or does that come later?"

"There's nothing glamorous about investigation. It's hard work." The mustard from his sandwich dripped on his shirt. "Oh, shit." He dabbed at it with a napkin.

He got up and went into the bathroom. I heard water running.

"You need some help?"

"No, I can clean a shirt by myself. But the napkin maneuver made it worse."

When he came back into the room, he wasn't wearing a shirt. And he looked good. He had broad shoulders and sculpted abs covered with light hair.

"I can call Jacque and get him started on the Massachusetts corporation. He and his sisters can track down anything."

Troy put on a clean shirt. "See, you can do the glamorous investigative work too."

"This is what I do all day. Make phone calls, follow up, collect paper. It's not what I went to law school for."

"It's the stuff of police work too. I guess if they told you in law school or the police academy how boring most of the work was, nobody'd do the jobs."

"You went to the police academy?"

"Long time ago. Old news." Troy finished buttoning his shirt.

I finished my sandwich and called Jacque.

"Land here."

"You sound so formal."

"Didn't know whether this number was still assigned to you."

"Assigned to me?"

"You're on a phone that rings in as Commonwealth of Massachusetts. You're not working anymore, so I wasn't sure it was you."

Damn. Never considered the phone. Now whoever read the phone bill knew where I was and who I called. And I'd probably have to pay the roaming charges, as a state-issue phone only covered area codes in the state.

"You didn't even think of that, did you, sugar?" Jacque chuckled. "You ain't no spy at heart."

"Okay, I'll never make it as a spy. That's what I need you for." I gave him the information about Deer Lick Conference Center, Inc. and hung up the phone.

Troy put his arm around me. "Don't worry. I didn't think of the phone either. You can use our own mobiles from now on."

He removed his arm from my shoulders. I missed it immediately.

Troy flipped open the laptop. "While we wait, let's see what we can get about the conference center online. If there's any service out here."

He found a recent article on Amanda Simmons, but the service died before he could bring it up.

Troy's cell phone rang. I recognized Jacque's home phone number.

I picked it up and answered it. "Hi, Jacque."

A child screamed in the background. Then a banging noise.

"Hi, sugar. I'm baby-sitting my nephew, so I haven't got much information for you. But the corporation was founded in 2002 with officers Sterling White, William Anders, and Amanda Simmons. Bought the center a few weeks later and haven't done much since then. Income from contributions about $45,000 a year."

"Yeah, we went online and got that info. Amanda Simmons works with Ames Dry Cleaning. I met her a few times at adoption events. Don't know the other two, though."

"Stop that right now!" I heard Jacque's phone hit something solid. More screaming in the background. Jacque picked up the phone again. "Child wants to go to sleep, so I need to make this short. All the contributions come from three people, each giving $15,000 a year. William Anders, Amanda Simmons—again, and Lemore Dinsmore."

"We met Dinsmore. He doesn't strike me as a philanthropist. Or someone that makes more than a few thousand a year."

"Well, he's given the money every year for the past five years. Got to go do the uncle thing. You take care, honey." And he was gone.

I relayed the information to Troy while I knelt on the floor and picked up the remains of our meal. I knew people hid information about charitable contributions but Dinsmore didn't strike me as the giving type. Petty larceny, maybe. Failure to pay child support. But not a philanthropic businessman. I rummaged in the papers on the floor.

"What are you looking for?"

"Dessert. A great meal like this should have dessert."

Troy walked over to his jacket on the bed. Out of the pocket he drew a dozen cellophane wrappers, each containing a fortune cookie.

"Let's celebrate with the cookies," said Troy. "Left over from my lunch a few days ago."

I put the cookies on the cleanest sandwich wrapper. "Why did you get so many of them?"

"In case I don't like my first fortune, I can have another. And if your first fortune doesn't say you'll fall in love with a handsome stranger, then you can keep picking new cookies until it does."

"When does this handsome stranger show up?"

"For that remark, I get the first fortune," he said.

He made an elaborate show of going through the cellophane wrapper, studying each and picking out a cookie. He broke the cookie in two, studied both halves, and slowly withdrew the fortune. He placed the piece of paper on the nightstand, smoothed it out, and placed it under the water glass. Holding the cookie between his index finger and thumb, he took a tiny bite. And then another.

"What does the fortune say?" I put my hand around the water glass.

He put his hand over the top of the glass to prevent me from lifting it. "In a rush to get to the good stuff? Let me finish the cookie first."

"The cookie may be the good stuff."

Troy didn't respond to my remark.

"What does it say?" I asked again.

"It says the events of this evening could change my life." He put the remainder of the cookie in his mouth.

"It doesn't." I took hold of the paper and pulled it from under the glass. Glanced at it. "That's what it says. Did you mark this one? Or do they all say the same thing?"

"No, they're different. Mine says this evening is life changing, yours talks about a handsome lover."

"Oh, you've gone from handsome stranger to handsome lover." I gazed at his lips. "Quick progression."

I picked out several cookies to study before putting them all back. Then took one, put it on the nightstand, and looked at Troy. He wasn't going to take the bait. Even if he was here all night, he wasn't going to ask me to open the cookie.

I placed the cookie in front of Troy. "You read my fortune."

"You trust me to tell you what it says?"

"No, I'll check it after you read it."

"It says *You will meet a tall stranger and fall in love.*"

"It does not. Give that to me."

Troy placed the piece of paper over the burning candle on the television. In one swift motion, I blew out the candle, grabbed the paper, and started reading.

"It says that my lucky numbers are 2, 7, and 8." I almost sounded disappointed.

"Yes, but any woman with lucky numbers 2, 7, and 8 always falls in love with me."

"I always considered 9 my lucky number. What's that mean?"

He took the cookie from me. "Sex, at the very least."

"Sex is the very least?"

Troy walked around the table and kissed me. His mouth was firm and warm and tasted like mustard and tomatoes.

I pulled away from him.

He picked up another cookie, broke it open, and handed me the fortune. "You read it."

"*You will be fortunate to have your lover with you in your old age.*"

Damn.

Troy stepped closer to me, lifted my hair, and kissed me like he meant it. His teeth played with my lower lip. While I enjoyed the warm feeling, this could get out of hand. I stepped back.

"Too soon?" Troy ran his fingers down the side of my neck.

"Too much."

"Glad I have that effect on you."

He sat on the bed. I sat next to him. Our hands were the only body parts in contact, but I still felt the burning sensation.

"Sorry about the bed." Troy leaned back.

"What about the bed?"

"It's the only place I can sit next to you. Is it too suggestive?"

I chose not to answer that question.

"You set the pace. We'll do it your way." Troy stroked my face again. "Will you stay or are you going back to your room?"

I looked around the generic motel room, with papers scattered on every surface. Not what I imagined for a romantic interlude.

Troy was a nice guy. I'd been with lazy men, controlling men, and clueless men. One more didn't make a difference.

That wasn't fair to Troy. This man reeked commitment. He searched for years for his children, he tried to do right by his ex-wife, and he occasionally played hero. Scared me to death.

Troy played for keeps. He had children and I didn't know whether I was ready for motherhood. Even step-motherhood.

"I don't know."

"Maybe I could persuade you."

He leaned in to kiss me. I drew back. He took both my hands in his.

"I'll stay right here until you tell me what you're thinking." Troy squeezed my hands. "You can go back to your room, but I wish you wouldn't. If you stay, I'm going to sit here until you talk to me."

Oh hell. I trusted him enough to leave the state with him. I admired him for who he was. Give him a chance.

"I've been married twice before—both ended in divorce."

Troy nodded.

"Brian, my first husband, couldn't keep a job, dropped out of school. It didn't last long."

He continued to look at me as if I were the most fascinating storyteller in the world. Had the silent thing down pat. He was a man of his word. He listened.

"Then I married Alvarez. After three years of marriage, and divorce, he's still Alvarez. Eduardo didn't seem to fit him. And never Eddy. He's ambitious and orderly and formal. And I can't believe I'm telling you this and I haven't had any alcohol to drink."

"I can run out and get something if it'll make you tell me more." Troy leaned in and put my head on his shoulder. "But I'd rather stay. You're afraid that if we get involved, I'll leave you too."

"That's not it." I brushed the corner of my eye, just to make sure there were no tears. "I know you're in it for the long haul. And you got kids. That much commitment is hard for me. What if I want to leave?"

Damn, I was going to cry. My sobs were the only sound in the room. Troy held me. No trying to bargain or saying I was foolish. Just a good, solid presence.

Troy offered me his handkerchief. White, about a foot square. Who carried a handkerchief these days? I blew my nose. Probably the least romantic thing I could do.

"You don't understand." But I needed to try to make him. "I've never been in a situation I couldn't leave. No pets, no kids. You come with baggage. And kids. That scares the hell out of me."

"Baggage and kids. I want you to be part of it."

"What if I want to leave?"

"What if you don't? We'll take it slow. You and me first, to see how that works out. Then add the kids later. Slowly, if you need it that way."

"What if I can't do it? What if I want to leave?"

"Let's see what happens between now and then. I've had relationships too. Some ended badly. Like with Margaret. But I still care about her. Just because a relationship changes over time, doesn't mean it's not worthwhile."

He kissed me. His hand went under my shirt and encountered the scar tissue. Softly, he explored every ridge and stitch.

"Please don't." It took all my willpower to back away again.

"Please don't what? Touch you?" His hand grazed the scar on my belly. "I thought you were enjoying it."

"Please don't pretend you don't see the scars."

"I see the scars." His hand moved to the horizontal one across my pelvis. "I just don't care. You've done some living, you've got scars."

Troy put his arms around me. "Tell me about the scars."

"Why do you care?"

"I care because they're important to you." He looked into my face. "Tell me."

Some men saw the scars and immediately pulled away. He got closer.

"Romantic, huh?" I tucked the handkerchief under the pillow. Wasn't going to hand it to him now. "You try to seduce me, I start to cry."

"Tell me about the scars." Gentle, but insistent.

I took a few deep breaths. "Plastic surgery. I had plastic surgery. A lot of it."

I turned to face him.

"Why did you have plastic surgery?"

I didn't know how to answer.

"This is a change in our relationship," Troy continued. "A change for the better. Please tell me what happened."

"I had gastric bypass surgery."

"You had your stomach stapled?"

"Jacque said that too," I smiled. "Made it sound like an office procedure. It's major surgery."

"Why'd you do it?" Troy sounded genuinely interested.

"I weighed almost four hundred pounds. Could barely move. As you can see, it worked."

Troy's hand moved toward me, then dropped to the bed. "And the plastic surgery?"

"After I lost the weight, my skin was hanging in folds from my body. Needed tightening. It's not uncommon. In fact, insurance paid for most of the plastic surgery because the extra layers made it hard to move."

"How long ago was this?"

"I had the gastric bypass about four years ago. Had the plastic surgery about two years back." Another deep breath. "Alvarez left just before the second surgery."

"The second surgery?"

"It's major surgery. First, they did the tummy tuck, horizontal and vertical. Six months later, I had my breasts and arms done."

Troy lifted the arm nearest to him. "Didn't even notice the scars on your arms. All the surgery is professional and barely noticeable.

"You are beautiful, you know." His fingers traced the line of my shoulder. "The scars just show you've done some living."

"I've tried hard to accept the scars." I sighed. "Sometimes it's hard." I turned around and kissed him. "But you're making it a lot easier."

His hands and lips caressed me. Down my whole body.

TUESDAY, NOVEMBER 9

Essex Hotel
Essex, Vermont
11:00 AM

I heard Troy in the shower. Went into the bathroom, pulled open the curtain, and joined him.

"Didn't want you to use up all the hot water, so I thought I'd join you."

Troy smiled. "Only in the interests of water conservation." He wrapped his arm around my waist.

"Hey, the thermometer outside the room says it's only 10 degrees outside. And I can't believe this place is generous with the hot water."

"There are other ways to heat up." Troy took the washcloth and ran it down my body.

A cell phone started ringing.

"Don't answer it," I said.

"I have to answer it." He got out of the shower stall and slid on the tile floor. His head hit the glass door and he swore. "Hope it's worth it."

I continued my shower and took full advantage of the hot water. The curtain opened again, and I prepared to welcome Troy back. But he didn't step into the spray. Naked man with cell phone—quite an interesting picture.

He held the phone out to me. "It's for you. Jacque."

"Welcome back." Jacque's accent was in full Caribbean mode.

"What do you mean, welcome back?"

"Honey, your suspension's been lifted. DA says he's not pursuing the criminal case. Course he added 'at the present time' as a CYA move. You start back day after tomorrow. Fast work."

"Thanks," I said. "How did the suspension get lifted? Is it automatic because of the DA's decision?"

"Don't know about automatic, but Ames's manager called Davis and told him that he needed you to do the adoption parties. Sounds like some financial pressure may have been applied."

"Amanda Simmons called Davis. That's interesting." I turned off the water. "Amanda Simmons is connected to the conference center and she got me my job back."

"Yeah, quite a coincidence."

I grabbed a towel and wrapped it around me. The air was cold after the hot shower.

"And we don't believe in coincidences, do we, Jacque?"

The phone beeped. "Jacque, I've got to go. It's Davis, probably to tell me officially."

"Be sure to act surprised." Jacque cut the connection.

Davis repeated what Jacque just said. Without mentioning Amanda Simmons.

I took a deep breath and told Troy. "We have one more day to explore up here." I was trying to make this right. "We can go out to the camp and look around like we planned."

Troy just stood in the middle of the room, pulling on his shirt. "Just one more day. I can't find my kids in just one more day."

"But I'm going back to work. I can't be with you anyway. And maybe the kids can be placed with you." I wasn't doing this very well.

"Yeah, maybe this and maybe that. I thought we were both going to find out where my kids are."

"We are." I tried to sound certain. "Just not in Vermont."

"But Vermont may be where they are. I'm going to keep looking." He picked up his phone and his wallet and put them in his pockets. "Let's get started."

"Hey, look on the bright side. At least I know about the remote starter and we can get into a warm vehicle." I walked to the window, opened the curtain, and pointed the remote starter at the truck.

The truck exploded in a burst of flame.

Essex Hotel
Essex, Vermont
11:55 AM

Even inside the hotel room, I felt the wall of heat. My hair and eyebrows burned. The window burst inward, covering Troy and me with sharp, tiny fragments. I threw up my hands to protect my face. It wasn't much protection.

Troy caught me as we fell to the floor. I smelled sulfur and felt blood trickle down my face and arms.

Troy's fingers probed my head and shoulders. "Lots of blood, but no deep cuts." He held up two fingers. "How many?"

"Two." I shook my head. "I'm dazed, not blind." I stopped shaking my head because it felt like explosions behind my eyelids. Thankfully, the pain stopped when my head did. "What about you?"

"I was standing behind you. Some cuts, but you got most of it."

I pulled myself up and sat on the bed.

"Don't move around too much. You've got a shard of glass in your leg," said Troy.

I looked down. Glass, about two inches wide and sticking six inches out of my skin. I laid back.

"Don't touch it," said Troy. "I'm calling 911."

"Somebody else probably did that already." I raised my bloody arm to eye level. I sat up but didn't faint. Troy was talking on the phone.

"The truck blew up when my girlfriend pressed the remote starter. We'll need an ambulance."

The rest of the conversation was lost to me. Pieces of glass fell off my clothing and out of my hair and I was trying not to get cut again.

Troy put down the phone, patted my arms, and unbuttoned my shirt.

"What are you doing?" I tried to pull the shirt closed. Somebody would be here soon.

"Just making sure you're okay. There's blood everywhere."

"Ouch." I pulled away from him. "It feels like thousands of tiny daggers."

"You're just lucky those daggers didn't take off something important."

It wasn't very funny, but I laughed anyway.

"What about you? Any cuts?"

"Something in my head." He leaned down toward me.

"I don't see any glass," I said.

Troy's cell phone rang. He ignored it.

"Aren't you going to get that? It might be the 911 people."

"The EMTs are in the parking lot. See the lights?" Troy went to the window, now empty of glass.

I attempted to stand up. And didn't make it.

"Just sit still and wait for the ambulance."

"Was anybody else injured?"

"I don't think so." Troy sat beside me on the bed. "That glass in your leg looks serious. Let's leave it for the EMT."

"Are you going to check the parking lot?"

Troy looked out the window frame. "Quite a crowd gathering." He went to the door and signaled someone. "I don't think I'm needed. I'll wait here with you."

I realized he was fighting his natural inclination to go to the rescue. Uniformed men entered the room.

They loaded me and Troy into the ambulance. Troy answered questions. I tried to stay upright.

I must have fainted, or took a short nap, because the next thing I remember is the emergency room. This was becoming a bad habit. Maybe I can write a travel guide to emergency rooms in New England.

I woke up to Troy and a police officer in the bay with me. "S. Yee" said the tag on the officer's chest, though he didn't look Asian. They seemed to be in the middle of a conversation.

"How'd your truck get to be such a mess?" asked Yee.

"My friend tried to start it with a remote starter." Troy gestured toward me. Friend didn't seem to come close to describing who I was. Troy's phone beeped.

"You gonna get that?" Officer Yee asked.

"Nope." It beeped again.

"What are the two of you doing in Vermont?" Officer Yee asked.

"My kids disappeared. My sister-in-law lives in Dummerston, led us here."

"Who's she?" Officer Yee gestured toward me.

"Helping me look. She works with children."

It seemed that Troy wasn't going to tell Officer Yee who I worked for.

"Sounds like you got a lot going on. Think somebody's out to get you?"

"I don't think it's random." Troy gave him the abbreviated version of how his children came to be missing. Without telling him about the custody proceedings in Massachusetts.

"Hope your girlfriend's going to be okay." Yee seemed genuinely concerned. "You too."

"I just needed some antiseptic cream and some bandages," said Troy. "She's the one with stitches. I'll contact you if I think of anything else."

"Here's the number." Yee handed him a card and left.

Without looking, Troy hit redial on his phone.

"Land? What are you doing on my phone?"

Troy pressed his phone and I heard Jacque say, "You called me, man."

"I just hit redial. It's Troy Higgins. You're on speaker phone with me and Niagara. Were you trying to reach me?"

"Just a minute."

Troy heard Jacque get up and close a door.

"I was trying to reach Niagara. She wasn't answering her phone."

Troy didn't hesitate. "We've got a situation here."

"What kind of situation?"

"Niagara's been hurt. She's in the hospital."

"What did you do to her?"

Troy gave Jacque the abbreviated version of the story.

"I'm on my way. What hospital?" Jacque didn't waste words either.

I saw Troy looking through the plate glass window into the emergency room. The nurse in charge of getting rid of annoying boyfriends was nowhere to be seen. He entered the revolving door just as I reached it, my shoes in my hand.

"Making your getaway?" He looked me over, from head to toe. I looked down at my arm, still covered with a sticky brown substance.

"It's disinfectant. They didn't want the cuts to get infected. Most of it was superficial. The painkillers they gave me helped."

"And do they know you're leaving the hospital covered in the stuff?" Troy looked down. "And without your shoes."

"I'm fine, no permanent damage." I bent over to put on my shoes and fell forward into his arms.

A police officer, dressed in the Deer Lick uniform, entered the ER. He looked at me being held up by Troy.

"Ms. Fontaine. Mr. Higgins." The local officer stepped between us. "Can I talk to you?"

"How do you know who we are?" Troy sounded like Alvarez. Or maybe it was just the painkillers they gave me.

"Saw you both at the crime scene. Guess you weren't paying any attention to me. I'm Officer Anderson." He walked up to the nurse in charge, recently returned from her important duties. "Mabel, can we use an empty conference room?"

Mabel smiled and pushed back hair the color of dirty snow. "Of course, you can, but the only empty one's on the second floor. 2D."

Her animosity didn't seem to extend to local cops. Maybe she just saw Troy as interfering. Anderson seemed to know where he was going. Troy and I followed him to the elevator, down a corridor, and to a tiny conference room with a round table and three chairs.

"You okay, miss? Can I get you something?" Anderson's concern seemed to make Troy uncomfortable.

"Officer Anderson, Ms. Fontaine is ill. Can this wait until later?"

"No, I'm afraid it can't. I just came from the crime scene. Brought in police officers from all over the state. Vermont's still rural, we need to rely on each other. You'll be glad to hear most of your gear's salvageable. Some of it smells like smoke, some has glass in it, but I think you did good. Of course, your truck is gone."

"But you didn't come over here to tell us this."

Anderson shifted in the chair. "No, I didn't. Can you tell me what happened before the explosion, Mr. Higgins?"

He went through the story again. Anderson took notes.

I could barely keep my eyes open. Troy droned on. Officer Anderson was staring at me. I didn't know why.

"Ms. Fontaine, can you tell me what happened?" Anderson flipped to a new page in his book.

My eyes closed. I tried to remember. Troy had stopped talking. It was quiet. Now it was my turn to talk.

"Officer, can't you see she's in no condition to talk?" Troy, to my rescue again. "I'm taking her home. You can question her later."

Anderson had some compassion. He flipped closed the notebook. "Okay, but I've got to talk to her soon."

Mabel, the ER nurse, was at the conference room door. She stepped in front of me and I collapsed into her arms.

"Who let this girl up and around?" Mabel scanned the conference room. "Raymond Anderson, did you tire her out with your jabbering?" Mabel didn't seem to expect an answer. She helped me to a chair. "There's a gentleman downstairs asking for you. Jacque Land."

I said the first thing that came to my mind. "How'd he get here so fast?"

Essex Community Hospital
Essex, Vermont
6:15 PM

Jacque paced back and forth across the ER waiting room. A deep frown marred his round, mahogany face. He came toward me before I had a chance to acknowledge him.

"Where the hell have you been? What happened to you?" Jacque's voice lost all semblance of an accent. Curious, that only happened when he was under stress. He enclosed me in a bear hug.

"I'm fine." It sounded insincere even to my ears.

"No, you're not fine. You have pieces of glass in your hair." Jacque leaned over and picked out a tiny shard.

"It's not very big." I took it from him and threw it away. "I thought I got all of them."

Several other people in the ER looked over, pretending not to be interested in the exchange.

"Can we go somewhere to talk?" Jacque looked around the ER.

"We were upstairs in a conference room." I crossed my arms like that made me more believable. "But I don't want to go up there again."

"In here." Jacque's talent for finding secluded spots to interview people did not fail him.

Troy followed Jacque and me into the alcove.

Jacque wasted no time on small talk. "Come back to Massachusetts with me. Now."

"Don't order her around." Troy spoke for the first time. "She's been through a lot."

"Because of you, flic." Jacque pulled him aside.

"What the hell is a flic?" asked Troy.

"French for a pain in the ass cop. I spent some time in Martinique," said Jacque. "It works for wannabe cops too."

I worked with Jacque for years; I knew flic was a not a very complimentary name for a cop.

The staring match between the two men was interrupted by Officer Anderson. He had more questions. Troy left with him. I sagged against the wall.

"Here, sit down." Jacque walked me over to a plastic orange chair bolted to the wall. "Can I get you anything?"

"Yeah, an explanation of what just happened. Why are you coming on like my big brother?"

"Because you need a big brother."

I just stared at him. Silence was a good weapon, but I just couldn't think of anything to say.

"Think, sister, think." Jacque sat in the blue chair next to me. "Who got you up to Vermont? Who got you to forget about poor, dead Scarlett to chase after his own kids? Who got you almost blown up?"

I was confused. There was something wrong with Jacque's argument, but I didn't know what it was. He almost made sense. Troy was on my side, wasn't he? He tried to include me in his search and he distracted me when I couldn't continue with the Scarletti case. Maybe Jacque was right. Maybe the medication was affecting me. I didn't know what to think right now.

"You don't have to think about it now." Jacque, once again, voiced my own thoughts. "We'll get you home, you go back to your job, and you can figure out what to do next." Jacque made a move toward me.

I thought he was going to pick me up. "I'm too big for you to carry. I'll walk."

"I could carry you if I had to."

"I need to say goodbye to Troy. Where is he?" I stood up and started in the direction that Troy and Anderson had gone. I found them standing in front of the vending machines.

"Troy, I'm going back with Jacque. I've got to go to work." Nothing like a bold statement.

"I thought we were going out to the conference center tomorrow? Look around."

"Conference center?" asked Anderson. "There's nothing out there."

"I got to concentrate on my job. Scarlett's murder." I found it difficult to pronounce the words. Maybe there was something wrong with my logic, but I couldn't figure it out here. I followed Jacque to the car and slept all the way home.

WEDNESDAY, NOVEMBER 10

1065 Main Street
Apartment 2C
Meredith, Massachusetts
11:10 AM

I woke to full sunlight, though it was a weak winter sun. I was home. I slid out of bed onto the cold floor. Then stumbled over to the thermostat and was rewarded with the roar of the furnace. Coffee, I needed coffee. No, I smelled coffee.

Someone else was in the apartment. Not likely someone broke in to make coffee, but I was careful. I peeked into the living room and saw Jacque sitting on the couch, watching CNN. I suppressed the sinking feeling when I realized it was not Troy.

"Good morning. Checking on the news of the world?"

Jacque didn't jump or otherwise acknowledge that I'd surprised him. "Morning. Want some coffee?"

I poured myself a cup. "Did you spend the night or come for an early morning visit?"

"You were out of it last night. Didn't even wake up when we got home." Jacque took a sip of his coffee. "And I spent the night. Again. The neighbors will talk."

"Let 'em. I was so exhausted I don't even remember coming into the house."

"You didn't walk in. I carried you." He smiled. "Told you I could do it."

"Well, seeing that you have things under control, what's next on the agenda?"

"Mr. Davis wants to see you this afternoon. At two."

"Today? He's in town on a Tuesday?"

"It's Wednesday, love. You've been asleep for a while."

"What time is it now?"

"Just after eleven."

I stared at the clock. "I've never slept this late or this long. But I do feel better."

"Well, make yourself beautiful because Davis is expecting you."

Department of Children and Families
Legal Division
45 Maple Street
Worcester, Massachusetts
1:45 PM

Jacque parked in front of the building. I stepped out of the car and Jacque walked with me into the building.

"You want me to come to the top floor with you?" His finger hovered over the buttons on the elevator.

"No, I can do this by myself. I don't want Davis to think I need an escort."

Jacque pressed the buttons for the second and the third floor. I missed him the moment he left.

Davis greeted me at the door and took me into the conference room. He shut the door. "We need to keep our voices down. Everything we say will carry."

I remained silent. I'd had the same office for the past year. In a money saving measure, all the offices on this floor lacked soundproofing. Even the discussions in the conference rooms, with their serious implications, could be heard in the surrounding offices. I wondered what Davis wanted to keep secret.

Cautious. Maybe he was just cautious, not devious. Boredom set in. I'd been doing this job for five years, knew the way it worked. But Davis was going over all the job duties and terms as if I were a new hire. I knew the way it worked.

Davis placed yet another stack of papers in front of me. "Now let's go over the terms of your probation."

I sat up, no longer bored. "What probation?"

"You've been on administrative leave because of your actions. Protocol requires that you come back on a work plan."

"Work plan?" I stood up. "I can't do my job on a work plan. So many hours of computer entry, so many hours of trial prep." I all but threw the papers down in front of him. "So many hours of desk duty and paperwork."

Davis gathered up the scattered papers and put them in a pile in front of him. He straightened the edges, so all the sheets lined up. "The customary probation period is six months."

"I'm not going to be on probation for six months. I just came back from administrative leave that I didn't deserve." I walked to the door. "This discussion is over until I talk to my union rep."

"Let's discuss this." Davis re-straightened the edges of the paper that hadn't moved from fifteen seconds earlier.

"There's nothing to discuss. I want a union rep."

"I said the standard probation is six months. I'm willing to reduce yours to a week." Davis crossed his hands on top of the pristine pile of paper. "It'll take at least a week to arrange a meeting with a union rep. This way, you can go back to work today."

A loud rap echoed through the room. Someone was determined to make noise on the flimsy door. I smelled talcum powder before I saw Melinda Cass in the window. Guess the flimsy walls didn't keep out odors either.

She opened the door, entered, and Ms. Cass used up the space in the room. "I need to talk to you." Her gaze started at Davis and turned to me.

I stepped forward. "I can't discuss the Scarletti case with you."

Melinda Cass did not respond. I kept talking before she recovered and started her barrage of words. "If you have any concerns, you should speak to your attorney. I'm not supposed to talk to you when you're represented by counsel."

"Nobody will talk to me about anything. You'll all be sorry."

Ms. Cass turned and flounced to the door. Hard to believe that 400 pounds of woman could flounce, but she managed it.

I completed my business with Davis, accepted the one-week work plan and agreed to start that afternoon. I went to my office and switched on the computer. My password had expired while I was gone, and I had to call the IT people to get a new one. The Department kept a master calendar for the office on paper; I went to check.

I walked around my desk and ran directly into Jacque.

"I need to talk to you." Jacque took my elbow, walked me back into my office, and closed the door.

"I'm tired of men escorting me where they want to go," I said. I opened my mouth to continue, but one look at the worry lines on Jacque's face made me sit down. Behind my desk. He wasn't in control in this office.

"I need to talk to you." Jacque sat in the only other chair.

"So, talk." I picked up a pen and tapped it where the desk calendar should have been. What happened to all my office supplies? It looked like somebody had removed everything portable from the office.

"Niagara, I'm worried about you. What's going on between you and Troy?"

"What the hell happened in this office? Where's my desk calendar, my stapler, and my yellow pads?" I started opening drawers, looking for missing supplies. How did anyone expect me to do my job without supplies? My file drawer was full. Probably nobody wanted to go through the years of training materials I had never thrown out.

Jacque sat up straighter. His worry lines deepened. "Don't change the subject. I'll get your supplies back. What's going on between you and Higgins?"

"I'm trying to do my job here." I pulled out the middle drawer and lifted out the two pieces of paper in it. "That's all I have in the drawer. No staples, no sticky notes, no pens. You'd think they never expected me to come back." I dropped the two papers into the drawer and shut it. "Didn't they expect me back?"

"That's what I'm trying to talk about," said Jacque. "What's been going on?"

"How does the lack of sticky notes have anything to do with Troy?"

"That's what I'm wondering. The whole office is talking about you and him disappearing together." Jacque crossed one leg over the other. Not an easy maneuver for such a large man. "He's still the father of children in our custody. It's still a conflict. I want you around for a long time. You need to be thinking straight."

"Straight? You're giving me advice about being straight?" I forced a laugh.

I folded my hands on the empty desk. Probably looked like a librarian. "I know what I'm doing."

"I hope so. You have a plan?"

"Yes, I do."

"Does your plan include Troy Higgins? Because if it does, it's still a conflict."

I sat back in my chair. Having people who cared about you complicated a life.

"You're right. My relationship with Troy is a conflict of interest." No need to tell Jacque they got closer in Vermont. Hell, with his connections, he probably already knew.

"Doesn't it bother you that you didn't have a relationship, reported a potential conflict of interest, and got suspended?" Jacque put his feet on the floor. "Then took off with him, had a real conflict of interest, and got your job back?"

"Maybe it's about the fact that I shot a man. Or did you forget about that?" Not that I could ever forget it.

"Be careful, sugar. There's something wrong with this."

I left Jacque sitting in my office, collected my files for the afternoon, and walked down the corridor. When I passed the conference room, the door was closed. Through the window, I saw Davis talking to Melinda Cass. Maybe it wasn't a conflict when Davis talked to a client, because he wasn't the one in court with her. I'd talk to him later, after Cass left.

I drove to the courthouse and checked my files. Only three matters. A motion for records, a continuance for a new trial date, and the Bartolli file again. Mrs. Bartolli had filed a motion for visits, stating that Waters was denying her the right to see her children. Remembering the last court appearance, and Waters' testimony about Mrs. Bartolli's statements, I was not looking forward to a rematch.

Attorney Warner waited for me at the top of the stairs. "I want Waters off the case. First, he lies about my client's statements and then he won't let her see the kids."

"I've got to talk to Waters. I just got back."

"Yeah, I heard you had a hard time. Conflict and all."

Conflict and all. Why was everybody concentrating on the conflict and not on the fact that I shot a man? Even if he may have needed shooting and was already out of the hospital. And in jail.

Even Warner was feeling sorry for me. I needed to straighten things out. But first, Waters. I found him smoking a cigarette.

I walked up to him. "I need to talk to you about the Bartolli matter."

He continued to smoke. I stood up straight and pulled back my shoulders. I was not fifteen years old and he no longer controlled my life.

"Attorney Warner says Mrs. Bartolli hasn't seen her children."

"She hasn't." He took a long drag on his cigarette and puffed out two smoke rings.

"She's entitled to visits." Nothing like starting with the obvious.

Waters stubbed out his half-burned cigarette. On the ground, not in the receptacle two feet away. "She didn't call, I didn't know where she was, she didn't get visits."

"What efforts did you make to locate her?" I opened the file to take notes.

"I called the number she gave me. It was disconnected. She knows where I am."

I pretended to jot down notes. Needed to respond to his arrogance but I needed him on my side in the courtroom.

"Not everybody goes out of their way to assist parents, y'know," he said. "Like you do."

I stopped writing.

"Heard you got in big trouble for it, too," Waters continued. "You never did know when to say no. Even shot a guy for him."

We were not going into this. He had been my social worker for only eight months, fifteen long years ago.

I closed my file. "You can explain what you did to the judge. This conversation is over."

I walked back into the courthouse and shuffled through my bag to get emergency rations. Only two boxes of raisins. I ate both.

Hoping to avoid any further conversations, I went directly to the courtroom. The hearing started almost immediately. On the day I least wanted to do a hearing, everything ran on time.

As it was Attorney Warner's motion, she went first. Mrs. Bartolli took the stand and Attorney Warner went through her efforts to contact Mr. Waters and how many times she'd left messages.

"Mrs. Bartolli, how long have your children been in the custody of the Department of Children and Families?" Attorney Warner picked up a piece of paper as she asked the question.

"About three weeks."

That wasn't bad. The Department was only required to do a visit once a month. No violation of regulations yet.

"And how many times, in the past three weeks, have you called Mr. Waters to request a visit?"

"At least twice a day. About thirty times."

If she was telling the truth, it was suspicious that Waters didn't get any of them.

"Did you do anything other than call Mr. Waters?" Warner continued.

"Yes, about ten days ago, I wrote him a letter, asking for a visit."

"Is this the letter you wrote?" Attorney Warner gave the document in her hand to the witness.

"Yes."

"And did you get a response?"

"Yes, a letter saying that he was unable to contact me, and I couldn't have a visit until we talked."

Attorney Warner entered the letters into evidence. I could have objected. But the fact that Waters documented his efforts to contact Mrs. Bartolli seemed to work in our favor.

"Mrs. Bartolli, where do you live?"

"Meredith, at the address on the letter."

"And your phone records all the calls you make, is that correct?"

"Yes."

Attorney Warner got permission from Judge Ramos and handed yet another document to Mrs. Bartolli. "Can you identify that document?"

"It's a copy of the calls I made."

"And how did you get this record?"

"Went to the Verizon place, they printed it out for me."

"And how many times did you call Mr. Waters?"

"Objection." Nobody had authenticated any of these records.

Attorney Warner was ready for the objection. "Your Honor, I have certified copies of the Verizon records."

"Overruled. The records may be entered into evidence."

"Yes, and I called Harry, Mr. Waters, a lot."

"How many times did you call the Department of Children and Families in October?"

Mrs. Bartolli looked down at the bill in her hand. "I called the Department's main number twelve times. I called Mr. Waters' extension fourteen times."

The clerk hurried in and conferred with the judge. A brief recess was called.

Waters followed me out of the courtroom and into the corridor.

"So, what are we going to do?" he said.

At that late hour, the courthouse was almost deserted. But I didn't want to have this conversation in front of an audience. We went into an empty conference room.

"What do you mean, what are we going to do?"

Waters took a cigarette out of the pack and put it in his mouth. "I don't have time to do twice weekly visits. It's too much trouble and takes hours to round up all the children and bring them to the office for a supervised visit."

"So, let mother have the children unsupervised. Or find a relative to supervise the visits." My exhaustion caught up to me.

"I can't do that. She'll just take them to her boyfriend."

"Then you'll have to do the visits."

Waters tapped the cigarette on the back of his hand. Good, maybe he'd drop this whole thing, give in to his nicotine craving, and leave me alone.

"I can't do twice weekly visits. I signed the kids up to change the goal to adoption."

"This is a fairly new case. What services have you offered to mother?"

"What services can I give her? A brain transplant? That she

should suddenly have insight and not take up with sex offenders? I don't think any services will help."

Something was wrong with that argument, but I couldn't figure it out in my present state. When in doubt, retreat.

"Harry, I'm too tired to have this conversation now. I want to think about this, and we'll talk tomorrow. Go have your cigarette."

"I hoped you, of all people, could understand that sometimes things are not what they seem, and people get accused of things they didn't do." With that, he was gone.

QuikMart
Meredith, Massachusetts
7:15 PM

I stopped at the QuikMart on my way home. Not on my plan, but the car seemed to go there on its own. I bought chips, salsa, ice cream, and Snickers bars. For coffee, I pulled into the drive thru window at Dunkin Donuts. Ordered a large black coffee and donuts. The kid at the window looked half asleep.

"Rough night?" I asked, hoping someone shared my misery.

"My feet hurt. I've been here ten hours." The kid handed me the coffee. "And I spilled your coffee all over the front of my shirt."

The shirt looked like mine was not the first coffee spill. I tried to be friendly, but the kid gave me much more information than I could handle.

"Maybe it'll get better. After ten hours, you must be going home soon."

"Not soon enough." The kid wiped his hand across his nose. "That'll be $7.35."

"What about my donuts?"

"Donuts? Didn't I give you your donuts?" The kid leaned out of the window, as if I regularly hid donuts in my car. "Guess I forgot. Just a minute."

He wiped his hand across his nose again and picked up half a dozen donuts and put them into a box. Maybe I didn't want the donuts.

"Skip the donuts, I changed my mind."

"Sure you don't want something to go with the coffee?" Now the kid turned into a salesman.

"No, just the coffee." I paid him.

My phone beeped. A text message from Davis, the general counsel. I pulled into a parking space and took a sip of the coffee. Ames called an adoption meeting for tomorrow morning at 8 AM. Tomorrow was a holiday, Veteran's Day. But Davis said I was required to attend.

I drove to my apartment, made sure the door was locked, and

dived into the food. I started with the healthiest choice, chips and salsa. I felt the familiar burn in my solar plexus. I threw away the rest of the food.

THURSDAY, NOVEMBER 11

Department of Children and Families
Legal Office
45 Maple Street
Worcester, Massachusetts
7:52 AM

Ms. Simmons rose from her seat when I entered the conference room. She was almost six feet tall but wore high heels that probably cost more than my weekly salary. She wore a beige suit, pearl earrings, and had her white blond hair swept back from her face. She extended her hand.

We shook hands and I wished I'd spent more time on my appearance.

I sat down, as did Simmons, who opened her leather portfolio.

"Now, I wanted to meet with you about the children for the adoption party at the end of the month. About half of the children attending are over the age of eight." Simmons extracted a piece of paper from her portfolio. "Yes, here it is. Two children over the age of fifteen, twelve children in the eight to fifteen range, and seven children under seven."

Simmons slid the paper across to me. "Mr. Ames wants to know why there are so few younger children scheduled to attend."

"The list reflects our demographics." I had given this explanation twice already. "Most of the children waiting for adoption are school age or older. We generally have no problems placing infants and young children. And mothers voluntarily giving their children up for adoption, again, primarily infants, generally don't deal with us."

Simmons pursed her lips. "Mr. Ames understands that. But, for publicity purposes, he would like his picture taken with younger children."

Mr. Ames needed good publicity. That was the purpose, for him, of the adoption party. I kept my mouth shut. He did contribute a great deal of money, and he didn't have to. I needed to remain on Simmons' good side because I had some questions too.

"Publicity will make this event a success," Simmons continued. "I've discussed this with your General Counsel, Mr. Davis. If we show pictures of young children, more people interested in adoption will attend. Once they are at the adoption party, they can be introduced to the older children."

"Don't you think it's unfair to the older children to raise their expectations if people are not looking to adopt?"

The fallout after an adoption party was sometimes severe. Older children, rejected yet again, started acting out in school or attacked their caretakers.

"It's just good publicity. The younger children draw the crowds, the older children benefit also. I have statistics to prove it. And, as I said, it's already been approved by your General Counsel."

"I will ask again about younger children freed for adoption." I gathered the papers together. "Can you start the publicity with the children already identified?"

"Guess I'll have to."

I felt the disapproval roll off Simmons in waves. "Can I ask you a question about another matter?"

"Yes, you can ask. I don't know if I can help."

"Why is your name on the deed to a deserted camp in Vermont?"

Simmons hand stopped, for an infinitesimal second, on its way across the table. "A deserted camp in Vermont?"

"Yes, in Deer Lick, Vermont. You're listed as one of the corporate officers."

"Oh, that. Mr. Ames wanted to set up a charitable camp for children. He purchased the property at a good price and I agreed to put my name on the incorporation papers."

"But that was several years ago," I stated. "Why hasn't it happened?"

"Money. We still need to do more fundraising before the camp can be refurbished and opened." Simmons walked to the door. "It would be most unfortunate for the children if the camp opened and then had to close because of lack of funds."

Most unfortunate.

1065 Main Street
Apartment 2C
Meredith, Massachusetts
11:00 AM

I left work. Couldn't deal with other people anymore. Hell, I couldn't deal with myself. I was talking about adoption parties, which I hate doing. Not talking about missing children or shooting a man or a murdered child.

Fortunately, Gary LaValley, the man I shot, would be okay. I shot him in the leg with the first bullet, missed with the second, and knicked his face with the third. Hope I gave him a permanent scar. *No, I don't…Yes, I do.*

I debated with myself about continuing shooting classes. A gun stopped something worse from happening, but my gun also hurt another person.

Then my thoughts turned to Troy, his missing children, and who killed Scarlett and why.

I turned on the television and watched reruns of *NCIS* and *Law and Order*, even *Starsky and Hutch*.

After six hours of television, I still felt miserable. I had to sleep.

FRIDAY, NOVEMBER 12

Department of Children and Families
Legal Division
45 Maple Street
Worcester, Massachusetts
10:35 AM

I waded through endless paperwork. Was almost glad when a phone call came about a drug raid at a local public housing project.

"And you are?" I took out my yellow legal pad and two pens.

"Petra Adjudhar. I'm the Emergency Response Worker."

"What happened?"

"Drug raid at Ridge Hollow. Went from apartment to apartment and picked up at least four sets of parents with twelve kids."

I wrote furiously. Of course, the social worker was going to prepare an affidavit, but I always took my own notes. Gave me a sense of the matter. A shadow fell across my writing surface. Evelyn McMasters, my immediate boss, had entered my office.

I held up my hand to ask her to wait. McMasters' hand covered my pad and she mouthed the word "now."

"Hey, Petra, can I put you on hold for a minute?" I asked. "Another emergency just walked in."

I pressed the hold button.

"Is that one of the drug raid cases?" McMasters waved her hand in the general direction of the phone.

"Yes, Petra Adjudhar called to tell me she's filing in court today."

"Transfer the call to another attorney."

"What? I can do it."

"I have another assignment for you. Transfer the call to Chu."

McMasters waited while I arranged the transfer.

I hung up the phone. "So, what is it you want me to do?"

"From now on, you're in charge of the 29B hearings. All of them."

"29B hearings?"

"Yes, the yearly reviews of all the children in placement."

I knew what a 29B hearing was. Federal law, the Adoption and Safe Families Act, required that the court review every child placed at least once a year. This involved collecting forms, getting them signed, and putting them before a judge for approval.

"Collecting reports and doing federal forms? No trial work?" I wanted to make sure I heard correctly.

"We need an experienced attorney," McMasters said. "Doing the reviews in a timely manner means significant federal dollars to the commonwealth."

"I thought each attorney did the reviews on their own cases. The assigned attorney knows the matter best." I struggled to sound calm and competent.

"New procedure. From now on, you'll be doing all the reviews. We need one person with expertise in this area. Everybody's watching this." McMasters picked up my stapler and studied it. "You'll also be doing the birth certificates and notices of publication. Reassign your trial cases."

"Reassign my trial cases? Why?"

"I want you to concentrate on the reviews and publication. We have a backlog." She exited the office.

Reviews, birth certificates, and publication. I was a trial lawyer. Without any trials, if I did as McMasters asked. What had I done since this morning to make her take away my trial schedule? Davis, her supervisor, had lifted my suspension and put me back in court. Now things were moving in reverse.

Another phone rang. My day seemed to be regulated by bells and whistles and things I had no control over.

"Niagara Fontaine."

"Hello, Ms. Fontaine, this is Lois Smith."

The woman spoke as if she knew me, but the name didn't seem familiar.

"Lois Smith, from Meredith Mills. I found your purse in the waterwheel at the mill."

"Yes, Ms. Smith. How can I help you?"

"This is most unusual, but I think I can help you."

Smith's voice, clipped and professional, brought up an image of her sitting ramrod straight in her chair, solving the problems of the world.

"Most unusual, twice in a few weeks," Smith continued. "But we found papers with your name on them."

"Papers with my name on them?" I wasn't sure I heard correctly. "Where did you say you found them?"

"In the waterwheel. A briefcase caught in the waterwheel. Nothing gets caught in there for months. Now two bags in a few weeks, both with your name on them."

I looked down at my briefcase, on the floor by her desk. It was the only briefcase I had ever owned. Alvarez bought it for me when I graduated from law school.

"Ms. Smith, my briefcase is not missing. Are you sure it's mine?"

"No marking on the case," Smith explained. "And, of course, the contents were damaged by the water. But there are half a dozen official-looking pieces of paper with your name on them. Your signature is washed away, but it's your name typed at the bottom of the page."

Smith seemed sure of herself. Niagara Fontaine was an unusual name and unlikely to be mistaken.

"I'll be right over."

Department of Children and Families
Legal Division
45 Maple Street
Worcester, Massachusetts
11:25 AM

Jacque and Troy were in the waiting room when I left. Talking quite loudly.

Troy lowered his voice when I stepped into the waiting room, but I heard him clearly. "Don't appreciate what you did, taking Niagara from me at the hospital and bringing her back."

"Didn't appreciate you taking her to Vermont."

"I can protect her."

"So can I."

Jacque put up his hand. "Okay, you got the gun, you win." He sat down in one of the plastic molded chairs along the wall.

Troy put his hand where a weapon would be, if he were wearing one. "What do you mean, I win?"

"Isn't that what you want? To win? Okay, you did it."

Troy sat down across from Jacque. "No, I didn't win. I still don't have my children with me."

"Everybody's looking for your kids. We find them, they'll go to you. End of discussion." Jacque did his best to look menacing. He wasn't very good at it, but his large size was formidable.

"How are we going to work this out?" asked Troy.

"Shouldn't you be having this conversation with Niagara?" Jacque gestured to me and left the room.

I took a deep breath and walked toward a conference room. I was not having this conversation in the waiting area. Troy followed me in to a tiny room, just large enough for a table and two chairs. A third chair was folded against the wall, but nobody could move if someone sat in it. I stood and faced Troy.

He was good at using silence, but I was better. He spoke first.

"I still need to find my kids," he said. "And I need your help."

"No."

"But you and Jacque have the connections I need. Not to mention the Department has custody of my missing children."

"No."

"Why? Don't I deserve more than just a no?"

"No is a complete sentence." Great, now I was channeling Alvarez. But he did deserve some of the truth. "I'm struggling to keep my job and now my caseload has been reassigned. And I'm struggling to keep my license to practice law, which could be pulled if I talk to you without counsel."

"But you spent the last few days helping me."

"Maybe I was being stupid." Maybe didn't cover it. "But I'm smarter now."

I made a dramatic exit out of the conference room and back into the office. The receptionist behind her bulletproof glass told Troy that he could not enter the office without an escort.

Then I remembered I was on my way out when I met Troy. Nothing to do but wait. I watched the security camera until Troy left, then waited another fifteen minutes before I went to my car.

Meredith Mills
One Logan Place
Meredith, Massachusetts
11:55 AM

I pulled my car into the wind-blown parking lot. A breeze off the river created dust devils of sand. Since my last visit, the vegetation around the parking lot had died. With the barrenness of November, the Meredith Mills building looked more forlorn.

Lois Smith was at her post behind the Plexiglas barrier. She looked up at me and smiled. "Good to see you again." Smith did seem to mean it.

"Thank you for calling me. The papers you found may be important."

"Maybe. But they are a mess." Smith picked up a black garbage bag, propped against the back wall, and handed it to me. "I put it in here because it's still wet. Didn't want everything a mess."

"I appreciate you calling me."

Smith picked up a folder on her desk. "Only some of the papers were readable. Dried these out and some had your name on them."

I sat in the tiny reception area, pulled the folder from the garbage bag and opened it. Adoption petitions with my name and identifying information on them. Petitions for children I never heard of. Original adoption decrees for the children, complete with court seals and certification. All dated within the last six months. I only did a couple dozen adoptions a year. A dozen decrees and I recognized none of them. Somebody was using my name and credentials.

I went back to the receptionist.

"Can I see the waterwheel?"

The waterwheel was in or near the water. Brown, rapid river water. Deep water. Like the water I'd avoided my entire life. Or at least my life since my brother drowned.

"The waterwheel?" Lois Smith hesitated only a second before she made a phone call. "Joel will be here in a few minutes. He's got keys and can take you down there."

The memory resurfaced. I was six years old again. I felt the cold, dirty water closing over my head. I kicked my brother away and rocketed upward, gulped air, and swam to shore. I dragged myself out of the pond without my brother Ricky. He'd tried to cling to me, but I kicked him away.

I shivered. That was then. I needed to talk to somebody about the waterwheel now.

Instead of the greasy, disheveled man I'd expected, a tall, thin, immaculate man appeared. About fifty, Joel wore tan pants and a matching shirt that was starched and pressed. The stitching over his pocket said "Joel."

"You want to see the waterwheel, miss?" Despite his dapper appearance, he smelled of diesel fuel.

"Yes, can you take me to see it?" I stood up. "And answer some questions for me?"

"I'll do my best. But you know the wheel doesn't do much anymore, nobody goes down there."

"My things keep turning up there." I gestured toward the garbage bag and the folder leaning against the chair.

"You're Niagara Fontaine." Joel held out his hand. "Pleased to meet you."

We shook hands. Joel picked up the bag and placed it behind Lois' desk. I followed him down a flight of stairs.

I could hear the hum of machinery through the walls. It seemed we were going deeper into the factory, not toward the river. Not that I was in a hurry to get to the water.

"Have to go to the oldest part of the factory." Joel opened a door and stepped out into the parking lot.

We proceeded to a smaller building and entered through a door in the brick wall. Only one wall was brick; the rest of the building had white clapboards.

We entered a huge room with three sets of windows. A large tank overwhelmed the back wall. The smell of diesel fuel overpowered the river smell.

"This is the heart of the operation." Joel, sounding like a proud parent, went to a wall of dials and indicators. "The boiler that runs the whole factory is underneath us. Tanks hold thousands of gallons of diesel."

"I don't see a waterwheel."

"Wheel's down by the river, below the boiler. Factory was much smaller when it was powered by water."

I looked out the nearest window to the river. The dam, once painted industrial orange, was faded and rusted. About twenty feet below, water was pouring over the dam and rushing under the building. I stepped back.

Joel took a key from a nail on the wall and opened a metal door on the river side of the building. When we stepped through the door, the heavy rank odor of the river became stronger. Almost overpowered the diesel smell.

I could see the waterwheel below me. Made of metal, it was painted the same garish orange as the dam. I had expected a wooden wheel like the nineteenth century gristmill. This was an industrial tool.

Steep metal stairs hugged the side of the building. My boot barely fit on the narrow steps. I clung to the wall. This was a bad idea. I continued down.

At the bottom, I stepped off the stairs onto concrete. It was cold here, but I felt sweat fall into my eyes. Still inside the building, I looked directly down into the river. The water wheel, at least thirty feet in diameter, turned in the cold water.

Joel continued his tour. "This wheel used to provide power for the entire facility. Nowadays, it doesn't do much. But we can't take it out. The drives and axles continue under the entire building to the street. Have to tear down the entire place to get it out."

I pressed myself against the wall, as far from the river as the narrow space would allow. The concrete wall was rough under my hands. My feet froze, even with the boots.

Calm. I needed to remain calm. It was only water and there was little chance of falling into it. Joel walked confidently on the narrow ridge.

"Are you okay?" Joel asked.

I hadn't moved. Took a deep breath.

"I'll be okay." I took a tiny step away from the wall. "How do things get caught in the waterwheel?"

"Doesn't happen often. Most stuff floats right on by in the river. Occasionally, something thin, like your purse, gets stuck between the paddles of the wheel."

I looked at the wheel. Like the wooden model in my memory, it had paddles about a foot apart. Something would need to be narrow to be wedged in there.

"What about the briefcase? That's quite a bit thicker than my purse."

"Yeah, that's strange." Joel scratched his head. "Most stuff gets stuck was dropped in the river by accident. To get the briefcase close enough, somebody would have to stand right outside the building. Deliberately throw it over the dam. Doesn't make any sense."

Lots of things didn't make sense. Like how my name got in the briefcase that was thrown off or over the dam.

"How do you get the stuff that's stuck in the wheel?"

"With this." Joel picked up a long pole with a hook on the end. "Just hook it and pull it out."

I stepped back against the wall. "I've seen enough." My footsteps clanged all the way up the stairs.

Kara Salem started in without saying hello.

"Niagara, I've got more information on the Miller children. They're really gone."

The Miller children. Oh, yes, Judge Hartwell had returned them to their mother's custody a few days ago. Then the mother left with the younger children, and Annie Miller, the fourteen-year-old, had come to Kara for a place to stay.

"Now what?" I realized my voice was sharp and tried to correct it. "Do we need to take custody of the children?"

"No. Yes. I don't know."

That about covered the options.

"Take a deep breath and tell me what happened." I grabbed my legal pad.

"Annie's in our custody now. She's living with her paternal grandmother." Kara stopped for a breath. "Today, Annie got a letter from her mother saying she was in trouble and that the two younger kids were taken from her."

"By another state agency? What state is she in?"

"Not sure. The letter is postmarked Keene, New Hampshire."

I heard paper rustling. Probably Kara taking the letter out of an envelope.

"The letter says that somebody came and took the children from her. Somebody she calls 'The Big Man.' She doesn't know where they are."

"What do you want me to do about it?" I was at a loss as to how this involved me. Though I was concerned for the children.

"Mother's back in Massachusetts for the day. She wants to talk to us."

I figured I wouldn't be gone from the office for long. Probably wouldn't even be missed. I could do the reviews later.

"Where is she?" I asked.

"She's on her way to the office. She'll be here in about half an hour. Shall we come up to your office?"

Not a good idea. "No, reserve a conference room, I'll come over to your office."

I'd still be on Department property and I could make some inquiries about the kids on the 29B review list while I was there. Sure beat more paperwork. On my way out, I passed the conference room. Jacque was talking to Amir Alcindor, our intern. I waved as I walked by.

Department of Children and Families
Area Office
One Gold Street
Meredith, Massachusetts
4:00 PM

The receptionist buzzed open the door and waved me through. So much for security in a government building. Kara met me just inside the door.

"I've got Mrs. Miller waiting in one of the outside conference rooms," Kara said. "She visited Annie at her grandmother's and scared the hell out of her." I balanced the legal pad on the crook of my arm and tried to make notes. "What agency took the children? New Hampshire? That's Child and Family Services, isn't it?"

"The state didn't take the children. Mrs. Miller said some man did."

Kara opened the reception door. "Let's go talk to Mrs. Miller. I think you should hear it from her." Kara disappeared behind the door.

I followed her across the waiting area and into a conference room.

Mrs. Miller sat behind the table with her feet crossed. She wore a dress with a low neckline and a hem that barely covered her thighs. And for almost forty, her legs looked good, but her makeup was industrial strength. I saw the red rings around her eyes. She smelled like thyme.

I sat down. "Mrs. Miller, how can I help you?"

"My children are gone."

I remembered hearing that phrase from Troy. On him, it resonated anger and a definite plan to get his children back. Mrs. Miller just seemed defeated.

"Where are your children?" Kara asked.

"I don't know. Big Man took them." Mrs. Miller pulled a loose thread on the hem of her dress. It was cheap rayon and I feared that even less of Mrs. Miller would be covered if it let go.

"Mrs. Miller, we can't help you if you don't tell us the truth." I picked up my pen. "Tell us the story in your own words, starting with the night you left Annie behind."

"Didn't leave her behind." She crossed her hands over her breasts, pulling the dress even lower. "Can I have some coffee?"

Kara left the room to fetch the coffee. I needed her as a witness but figured a few minutes without Kara would make no difference.

Mrs. Miller waved her hand in the general direction of the door closing after Kara. "She don't believe I love my kids. She thinks I just left them."

"But you had a good reason." I leaned in toward Mrs. Miller. Grateful there wasn't a computer separating us. "What was it?"

"I didn't want Annie to do what I did and get in the trouble I got into. She's a good kid, real smart. First in my family to graduate from high school, if she makes it to next June."

"You have hopes and dreams for Anna."

"Damn right. She loves kids, she'd make a good teacher. Just don't want her to have a bunch of kids like me and get stuck on welfare."

"So you left her behind when you left?"

"Yeah, she gets education benefits as a foster kid. Maybe make something of herself." Mrs. Miller was looking all over the room, everywhere but at me. "Where's that coffee?"

"I'm sure Kara will be back in a minute with it."

Kara re-entered the room with coffee for all of us. I remembered Kara stating that one way to build trust is to eat or drink with the clients. I sipped my coffee.

Kara slid into the seat next to me. "So, Josie, where have you been for the last few weeks?"

"I needed a vacation. Too much shit going on down here." Josie sipped her coffee and made a face. "Bad coffee. You don't got a Starbucks around here?"

"Can't afford Starbucks on my salary." Kara smiled. "So, where you been?"

"Here and there. Mostly in Vermont."

I sat up straighter. "Where in Vermont?"

"Some godforsaken spot. No TV, no computers, rooms cold as ice."

"How did you get there?"

"I drove." Josie Miller twisted her coffee cup, first one way, then another. "I been there before. When my youngest, Michael, was born."

"What were you doing there then?" I asked.

"I was confused." The coffee cup twisted more erratically. "I wasn't sure I wanted another kid. The ones I got don't always get what they need." Tears appeared in the corners of Josie's eyes.

Kara got up and retrieved the tissue box on the windowsill. She handed Josie a tissue and put her hand on her arm. "I know it's hard. Who do you know in Vermont to help you?"

"I heard about this guy. He lets you stay at this place, rent free, while you decide what to do. No sex or anything." Josie blew her nose, a loud noise in the small room.

She continued. "And, and…if you decide to give your baby up for adoption, you get to pick out the people who get him and get to talk to them and everything. Not like this place."

"So, you stayed there. Then what happened?" Kara handed her another tissue.

"It was nice. I got good food and a place to stay and my kids got to play with the other kids there. Even met Scarlett, the little girl what was killed. She helped me with Michael. It's too bad she died." Josie paused.

My mind raced. Scarlett was in the same place as the Miller children? The Miller children with other children who disappeared, supposedly for adoption, made sense. But Scarlett was dead and too old for most adoptions. How did that fit in? Mrs. Miller might have relevant information, even if she didn't know it. I put out my hand to stop Kara from asking the next question.

"How did Scarlett get there?" I asked.

Josie shrugged her shoulders. "Same as all the other kids, I guess. Her mother brought her."

"Bella was there also?"

"Yeah, and she was pregnant too, with a little boy just like me. We both kept our babies, but it was a nice place to stay while we was pregnant. 'Cept for no TV and no computers."

Kara stared at me over Josie's head. She leaned back in the chair, waiting for me to ask the next question.

"So why did you go back to Vermont?"

"I'm getting evicted anyway. Though, seeing as I had custody of my kids, I could take them where I wanted. Went back to the place we stayed, but nobody was there. So, I...the place was unlocked, and I went in to stay with my kids. It was warm and all and I bought food."

I doubted the cabin was unlocked. And it still didn't explain how she met the Scarlettis.

Josie wiped her eyes. "And then the man came and said I couldn't stay there if I wasn't pregnant. And he gave me only a day to move and I didn't have no place to go."

"What happened?" Kara asked.

"He came back the next day, and I was still there. He took my kids. Both Mike and Bruce. Mike's a baby, and he needs me, and Bruce is just three and just started day care and I don't know where my kids are." She cried loudly.

"Where is this place?"

"White River Junction, Vermont. I don't know the address, but I know how to get there. But it's no use, my kids are gone."

"And the Scarlettis were there also? How big is this place?"

"No, I saw Scarlett at the other place. The cabin I stayed in only had two rooms. It was crowded with all my kids. But Bella and her kids were in the big place up the road."

"The big place up the road?" I echoed back the last phrase.

"Yeah, it was a big place, lots of buildings, about a half-hour drive from my cabin. Not that I ever drove there, somebody always came to pick me up. Only went there a couple of times, but Bella, Scarlett, and Amber were all there."

"Why did you go from your cabin to this place?"

"That's where they talked about adoption and giving up your baby. Most of the girls at the big place were about to deliver their babies and they all wanted to give them up for adoption. You didn't go there until the end."

"Do you know where this big place is?"

"No." Josie looked at Kara. "Can I have some more coffee?"

Kara left the room.

"I don't want to talk in front of her," Josie continued. "She thinks I'm a bad person because I thought I'd give up Mike."

I doubted that statement but waited to see what she said next.

"I'm not a bad person, just confused. And I don't know where the other place is. They always took me in a van or a car with tinted windows and I had to tend to Bruce, and he was always getting into things and I couldn't pay attention to where we were going." Josie took a breath. "It was on a dirt road, though, and everybody called it Camp Good News."

"And Bella was there? Even though she didn't give up her baby for adoption either?"

Josie's brow creased, and she scratched her head. "Yeah, that did seem strange. Though I didn't know she kept her baby 'til I read about Scarlett's murder in the paper and saw she had the baby with her."

Kara re-entered the room, followed by General Counsel Damon Davis.

"May I see you in my office?" Davis asked me.

"I'm in the middle of an interview." I gestured toward Mrs. Miller. "This woman has some important information."

"I'm sure Ms. Salem can finish the interview. I need to see you now."

Department of Children and Families
Area Office
45 Maple Street,
Second Floor
Worcester, Massachusetts
4:05 PM

I followed Davis into an empty office. Davis didn't engage in pleasantries. "What the hell were you doing just now?"

"Conferencing a case with the social worker. It's done all the time."

"Not by you." Davis pointed his finger at me. "You've been assigned to permanency reviews. Or didn't Ms. McMaster make herself clear?"

My hands bunched into fists. "You made yourself clear. But I was the assigned attorney on the Miller case and Kara wanted to talk to me. It was easier than starting over with another attorney."

"Sit down."

Davis sat and waited for me to do the same.

"I'm trying to be reasonable," Davis began. "I assigned you to reviews. If it isn't enough to keep you busy, I can find other work for you."

"I would like other work. I'm a trial lawyer. Give me some trials."

Davis shifted the documents on his desk. "That's not possible. It's better for the office if you don't do trials at the present time."

"Why?" I let the question hang in the air.

"Your personal life has become somewhat of a problem."

I remained silent.

Davis continued. "Not enough of a problem for disciplinary action or suspension, but it is better for the Commonwealth if you're not in court now. You shot a man."

"Better for the Commonwealth." I worked hard to keep my tone neutral.

"Better for you too. Now go back to your office and I will get someone to deal with the other situation."

Department of Children and Families
Legal Office
45 Maple Street
Third Floor
Worcester, Massachusetts
4:45 PM

Jacque was still in the conference room with Amir, the intern, when I returned to the office. He signaled to me when I entered the reception area. I went over to the door.

Amir wore black and gold sweats, several sizes too big for him. I suspected they were gang colors but didn't know whether Amir was in a gang or wanted to be or was just trying to mimic the latest fashion.

"So, Amir, what have you been doing?" Jacque asked. He turned to me and added, "Amir says he'll talk to you about what he knows."

"I got information," said Amir. "But I don't know that I want to talk about it here."

"We already went through this," said Jacque. "I can help you get off the street, where you weren't doing too good anyway."

"I was doing okay." Amir leaned back and put his sneakers on the table.

"Get your feet off the table." Jacque pushed them to the floor. "How do you know about the kids disappearing?"

"Why can't I put my feet up on the table? Not like it's clean or anything. People been carving their names in it since 1964."

"What the hell do you know about 1964? Just keep your feet on the floor. It's polite."

Amir made a show of resettling himself, feet firmly on the floor.

Jacque tried again. "So, what do you know about the missing kids?"

"What missing kids?" Amir looked at the floor.

"Are we going somewhere with this conversation or do you just want to walk it around?"

Amir leaned forward. "What's it worth to you?"

"You know I haven't got any money. What do you want?"

"Want to get off probation. Can you pull that off?"

Jacque turned to Amir. "So, you reformed?"

"Nah, just my probation officer says he'll get off my back, like he's supposed to, in three months. But I got this internship and I'm trying to get a job, so I don't have time to do probation."

"Okay, information's as good as you say, I'll see what I can do."

Amir settled himself further down in the chair. "So, see, kids are disappearing all over the place. There one day, gone the next."

"I know that."

"Then you're one of five people that does. This been going on for over a year now. Pregnant women disappear, have babies, come back without babies."

Jacque remained silent. This was interesting. Amir and Alvarez seemed to have the same information.

"Sometimes, women sell their little kids. Got to be under two, though."

"Sell them to who?"

"Ain't it whom?" Amir waved his hand. "Don't make no mind, the little ones get adopted by rich white couples. Mostly down in Boston."

"But Massachusetts requires that every non-relative adoption go through an adoption agency," I said.

"Ain't that way in other states."

Strange that Amir would have that piece of information.

"That's true," I confirmed. "They bring children from other states into Massachusetts?"

"Yup. With fake papers and fake names and everything. Got somebody with juice to forge documents." Amir sat up and stared at Jacque. "Heard say that a cop, one dating a lady DCF lawyer's in on it."

My training paid off. I don't think Amir picked up on my surprise.

"What DCF lawyer?" Jacque asked.

"Don't know." Amir shrugged. "Just heard they were in on it."

"How do they do it?"

Jacque and I looked through the conference room window and

watched Davis walk by. I decided to remain quiet while Jacque continued to talk to Amir.

"Mostly, the women volunteer. Get themselves knocked up and can't afford the kid, so they make a deal. Some of them make the deal before they get pregnant. Then they get sent out of state to have the kid. Get big bucks for a baby."

"Where do they get sent?"

"Different places. Hear the guy running the scheme's got money and has a bunch of real estate for the ladies to stay at. Screens them too. No drugs, no alcohol."

"So, you don't know where they stay?"

"No, but they got a bunch of companies. Twelve Apostles, Hair of Christ, they all got Bible names. And the paperwork talks about doing God's Work, finding homes for children and rescuing unwanted children and finding them good Christian homes, that kind of stuff. Don't know whether the dude really believes it though."

"Why don't you think he believes it?"

"Well, if he did, he'd go on TV or the Internet and say it. Not hide somewhere."

Amir's theory of celebrity and good works. You don't mean it if it's not on TV.

"About the forged birth certificates. Where do they come from?" I asked.

"I got your interest now?" Amir put his sneakers back on the table.

"You've got it," said Jacque. "Tell me what you know, and I'll try to help you."

"Dude in Jamaica Plains got a warehouse full of social security numbers, birth certificates. Stacks and stacks of them."

Amir gave the address to Jacque.

1065 Main Street
Apartment 2C
Meredith, Massachusetts
7:15 PM

Binge watching television was becoming a habit. Agent McGee of *NCIS* killed a man and I cried into a hand full of tissue. I know strong emotions go through cycles, but this was ridiculous. I shot a man who was trying to hurt Troy and me. Didn't kill him, used appropriate response to the threat. I didn't need a support group. I knew all the lingo. Still felt like shit.

And now my job was taken away from me. Not the whole job, but the best part. I loved being a trial lawyer, thinking on my feet. Good at it too.

A knock on the door. Damn Mrs. Schwartz for letting people in without knowing who they were. I ignored it.

"Niagara, let me in." It was Troy's voice. "I know you're in there. Your car is in the yard and all the lights are on."

This might solve one of my problems. Let him see me with bloodshot eyes and a stuffed nose. Might scare him away. If not, maybe my Wonder Woman sleep shirt and flannel pants with an unidentified stain would.

I opened the door. "What the hell do you want?"

He walked by me. Didn't even seem to notice me. Sat down in one of the armchairs. "I need to talk to you."

"Right now?"

"Yeah, right now. Can you turn off the TV?"

I sat on the couch and picked up the remote. Turned off the TV. Troy looked at me, the tissues, and the glass of Glenlivet.

"Did I interrupt something?"

"Yeah, I was entertaining all my friends." I gestured around the empty room. "And enjoying Scotland's finest." I took a sip of the Glenlivet.

"I'm sorry. But I need your help. My children are still missing."

Like that was my fault. One thing that definitely wasn't my fault. Man getting shot. Affair with father of DCF children. Richard drowning. Missing Miller children. Scarlet's death. Those were my fault. But not his kids.

"I need your help," he repeated. "I want to go back to Vermont and want you to go with me. I have a rental car."

Yeah, his truck was in small pieces in the Essex hotel parking lot. That may or may not be my fault. OK, I was being unfair. And wallowing in self-pity. If I kept on this way, I'd start whining.

"I can't go with you. I have a job."

"It's the weekend, Niagara. Give me two days."

"You can probably move faster without me." That might even be a winning argument.

"But I need you if I find the children. You represent DCF and they have custody. It would be a great help if you came with me. Two days only."

Or I could hole up in my apartment, drink whiskey, and cry.

"I'll be ready tomorrow morning," I said.

SATURDAY, NOVEMBER 13

I was on the way to Vermont again. With Troy. And a briefcase full of forged birth certificates with my name on them. They were still soggy from their time in the river, but my signature was clear on most of them. A very good forgery.

Troy's rental wasn't roomy, but it was available. Power windows but no GPS. We were using Troy's phone to navigate.

"Tell me about the adoptions." Troy's voice interrupted my thoughts.

He didn't look at me, just stared out the window. After the first few Vermont exits, the traffic was light.

"What do you want to know?"

"Why are the papers in the case, the ones with your signature, so important?"

"Because only the court is supposed to have decrees for agency adoptions. And they're supposed to be kept in a locked vault."

"Okay, for us slow learners, what's an agency adoption?"

That stopped me for a minute. My entire working life revolved around adoption and child welfare laws. I wanted to give Troy a good answer without all the legal minutia.

"Massachusetts is a state where all non-relative adoptions must be done through a licensed adoption agency. Only exceptions are set out in the law for grandparents, step-parents, aunts, uncles and other close relatives. People in the state can't make private agreements for adoption."

"And they can in other states?" Troy looked at me. He seemed genuinely interested.

"Yes, and it's quite common. The pregnant woman and couple who want to adopt make a private agreement. You see them on the internet and in magazines. 'Loving couple seek to adopt' adverts. Usually the adoptive couple pays the medical and living expenses of the mother. Then they adopt the child when it's born."

"What if the biological mother changes her mind?"

"That's a problem. She can't be forced to give up her child."

Musical notes from my purse. It's Jacque.

"Hey, girlfriend." I could hear children crying in the background.

"Where are you? Can you turn down the volume on that baby?"

"Sorry, there's a supervised visit going on and someone is not happy. Where are you?"

"Supervised visit on a Saturday? Isn't that unusual?" I asked.

"Special favor. Overtime too," said Jacque.

"In eight hundred yards, turn right onto the exit ramp." This from the mechanical voice in Troy's phone.

"In Vermont, almost at the Deer Lick exit."

"Let me get some place quieter." I heard footsteps and a door open and close. Jacque came back on the line. "Okay, I have some bad news and I think you are an idiot for going back to Vermont with Troy."

"How do you know I'm with Troy?"

The man in question took a right off the highway and pulled up to the end of the ramp. "Turn left" said the mechanical voice.

"You saying he's not there?" said Jacque. "Girl, I hear the mechanical voice and I know you can't drive and talk on the phone at the same time."

"I'm an idiot and I'm here with Troy." Sometimes the best way to deal with Jacque was just to agree with him. Especially when there were clear indicators that he might be right. "What's your news?"

"Had a meeting with Amir again. On probation, trying to get it right, but still connected with local gangs. His info may be iffy, but he says local lawyers are paying to counterfeit birth certificates and adoption papers. Sometimes even foreign adoption decrees for children not born in the U.S. Sorta vague on the details. Says somebody's making babies disappear too."

"Anything else?"

"Yeah, I looked over copies of the documents pulled out of the river. Seems like your name is being used for illegal adoptions."

"Black market adoptions?"

Jacque didn't answer immediately. I heard him talking to someone in the background. Looks like we're coming into Deer

Lick again. Several houses with tiny front yards; walk out the front door and hit asphalt. In a state as sparsely populated as Vermont, you'd think they'd have larger front yards.

"Looks that way." More voices in the background. "Got to go. Will let you know if I find out anything else." Jacque hung up without a goodbye.

"Black market adoptions?" This question from Troy.

"Yeah, they're illegal in every state. Adoptive couple pays for the baby above and beyond expenses. Buying and selling children. But it happens." I didn't want to go any further into that topic. "I'm cold."

"Don't change the subject. At least we got a steering wheel and the brakes work." Tory flipped a switch. "And the heater works. So, there's agency adoption and black-market adoptions and agreements to adopt?"

"They're called brokered agreements if there's some kind of broker setting it up. Usually through a lawyer or a minister or a priest. Though some people try on their own. Craigslist has a section for adoptions. Still not enough children and too many couples."

"That's why they're faking adoptions."

"The adoptions aren't fakes. All the documents we found in the briefcase were accepted as authentic and the adoptions went through. I know they're not real because my name is on them and I didn't do them."

"How'd they do that without you knowing?"

"I don't always go to the adoption. If all the paperwork's in order, and the court approves it, the adoption worker can handle the actual adoption. And everybody goes over the paperwork first. Don't want the adoptive parents showing up and it not happening."

"Who can do that?"

"Someone with access to state records, court documents, and a supply of children. Somebody with some juice."

"And Damon Davis is trying to keep you out of the way and out of the office."

"Yeah. There's that too."

Good News Conference Center
Deer Lick, Vermont
9:05 PM

Cold and dark. More cold and dark. When we arrived at the Good News Conference Center, the place looked deserted. And it had to be close to freezing. The buildings stood out in the gloom because they were whitewashed. Other than a few street lights, nothing was illuminated. No locks or gates barred the way.

Cold and dark but not silent. Even this early in the winter, I could hear my footsteps crunch under my feet. Troy, damn him, seemed to float over the landscape. Couldn't tell where he was by his footsteps, though I sensed him near. I tripped over some greenery and the brisk, woody smell rose from the ground.

"Thyme." I said it out loud.

"Time for what?" Troy whispered, though it looked like we were the only people here.

"Not time, as in a clock. Thyme, as in spice. It's all over the ground here."

"Don't see anything but frost."

"Not many places in New England with thyme growing in November." I bent down and pulled up a plant. "But it has a distinctive smell."

Troy took the plant and smelled it. "Like stew."

"One of its uses. Someone must be taking care of this, to be green so late in the season." I looked around the small patch, sheltered by the side of the building. "And, Gary LaValley, the man I shot, smelled like thyme."

"He's involved in this too?"

"Don't know." My foot slipped. "But we might find out."

We stepped into a cleared area in the center of the buildings. Some sort of courtyard. Probably a gathering place when the conference center was full. My heart sank. Over a dozen buildings ringed the central courtyard. Huge dormitories, built to house dozens of people, and smaller, intimate cottages for smaller groups. All probably full of closets and overhangs and thousands of other places concealing trap doors and hidden closets. The buildings could be connected by underground tunnels, for all we knew.

Troy took my hand and led me from the relative brightness of the common area, with its scattered street lights, into the dense darkness on the side of the largest building.

"What are you doing?" I whispered. I didn't know if anyone was here, but why take a chance? Buildings could be full of bugs and mice, and I didn't want to disturb them either.

"We're going around back of the buildings. Whoever is here is working hard to make it look deserted. Probably any lights can only be seen from the back." Troy was whispering also. "Or they're in the basement."

That made sense, and I had no better plan, so I followed Troy. No matter how hard I tried, every footstep made noise. Troy took out a flashlight and ran it over the ground. Somebody was here, judging by the number of footprints out back. One with work boots, one with sneakers, and a few sets of child size footprints.

"Don't want to attract attention." Troy turned off the flashlight and we were in the dark again. Now my footsteps really echoed.

The lock, rusted and old, gave way; no need for a lockpick. I moved closer to Troy. My eyes adjusted to the indoor darkness. I thought outdoors was dark, but the windowless room was black. Troy turned on his flashlight. It was a mudroom, with hooks on the wall and plastic trays lined up on the floor, ready for the boots in winter. There was a door beside me. I opened it.

The sound of a cartridge in a semi-automatic pistol is unmistakable. I froze where I stood. Seconds later, the lights in the room came on.

"Niagara!" That was Troy's voice.

The door slammed, and a lock clicked. Troy was trapped on the other side of the door. And I was trapped with the gunman. This had an ominous, familiar feeling. Only this time there was no way under the door.

The man with the gun had a navy balaclava over his face. Were his eyes black or was that just the shadows from the wool covering on his face?

"Do what I say, or I'll shoot. Can't miss at this distance."

I heard Troy pounding on the door.

"He's got a gun. Stay away from the door."

"Shut up. Or you're both dead." The gunman kicked me, and I went down hard.

I looked up when a second person entered the room. This person was enormous and dressed all in black. The outlines of a Kevlar vest stood out under the black turtleneck. These people were prepared for trouble. Each of them grabbed an arm and started dragging me toward the back of the room.

"Troy!" I had to let him know what was going on. "They're dragging me to the back of the room. One guy is short and the other is huge, over 300 pounds."

I heard Troy kicking the door. The large guy kicked me again—guess he didn't like the comment about his weight—and I passed out.

Good News Conference Center
Deer Lick, Vermont
Later that night

All was quiet. The deep, black silence of November in New England, far from the city. I felt the wooden floor under my cheek and heard voices. I didn't open my eyes.

"You kicked her hard? What were you thinking?"

"Doesn't matter, she can't see us and don't know who we are. And I didn't kick her that hard. She's only been out a few minutes."

"Okay, let's get her clothes off." Two sets of footsteps came toward me.

I rolled over and looked up. No way were they taking my clothes off without my having something to say about it.

"Look, she's awake. Told you I didn't hit her that hard."

"Good." The smaller person, now without a gun, helped me into a sitting position. "Now take off your clothes."

"What? No way." I was keeping my clothes.

"We need to search you for weapons and phones. Just strip down to your underwear and we'll pat you down. We'll give you your clothes back afterward." The smaller person backed away and picked up the gun. "Or I can knock you out and take off your clothes myself."

I didn't move.

"Take off her clothes." The smaller person signaled the larger one.

"Okay, okay, I'll do it myself." I took off my jacket and my boots.

"Faster. We need to get moving."

"Why such a hurry?" I did want to know, and I did want to delay the undressing.

"Get moving." Small had picked up the gun again. I finished undressing, down to my panties and bra.

"Guess you don't have a gun. And I'll keep your purse with the phone."

I watched Big go through my purse, repulsed as he checked my lipstick and tampon holder. Don't think I'll be using them. I felt a blow to my head and I passed out again.

Good News Conference Center
Deer Lick, Vermont
Later that night

I woke up in a tiny room. The couch smelled of cigarette smoke and the pillow was gray. I started coughing. Couldn't stand cigarette smoke, even secondhand in the upholstery. As my vision cleared, I saw a sink and toilet sitting against the wall across from me. Without getting off the couch, I could touch both fixtures.

But I wanted to get off the couch. Lying there, I watched bugs making their way across the surface. I sat up. Not a good idea. The headache radiated down my neck and onto my shoulders.

I thought of sitting on the floor but the gray cement blocks under my feet were sticky and cold. I'd take my chances with the couch. I leaned back on it and looked around the room. Eight-foot ceiling painted the same institutional gray as the walls. One tiny window above the toilet, one door at the head of the couch. A slot in the door, about fifteen inches long and six inches high. Big enough for a tray but not much more.

I lay back down, realized I was exhausted, and fell asleep.

Something woke me. Not the headache, though that was still present. A scraping sound. And a stronger smell of cigarettes. I sat up slowly. Better. Less pain this time.

"Hey, are you okay?" A female voice. Very young, late teens or early twenties. Not particularly stressed.

"Who's there?"

"I'm Fredricka." A giggle. "Well, that's my name here. I brought you some ice and some ibuprofen."

Two yellow stained hands came through the door slot, one hand holding two brown tablets and the other a commercial ice pack wrapped in a towel. I stepped closer and the cigarette smell grew stronger. Probably the source of the yellow stains.

I took both items. "Can I have some water?"

"There's a plastic cup on the sink. Use that."

I picked up the cup and rinsed it off. Hell, if I was going to take pills given by an unseen woman, why not drink from a dirty cup? I studied the pills—they looked like ibuprofen. And I needed to get rid of this headache or I'd be good for nothing. I swallowed the pills, laid down on the couch, and put the ice pack to my head.

"Thank you, Fredricka."

The giggle again.

"What do you mean when you say they call you Fredricka here?"

"We get to pick our own names," Fredricka responded. "And it's so much nicer than Betsy or Gertrude or something. What's your name?"

"Niagara."

"Like the falls?"

"Yeah, like the falls."

"How far along are you?"

I tried to concentrate. Maybe the blow to my head affected my hearing. "How far along what?"

"How pregnant are you?" Fredricka responded.

"I'm not pregnant."

"Isn't that why you're here? Isn't that why you fainted?"

"I didn't faint. I was knocked out by a gun butt." I made the blunt statement to see what reaction I would get.

"My mistake," whispered Fredricka. And she was gone.

SUNDAY, NOVEMBER 14

Good News Conference Center
Deer Lick, Vermont
About dawn

Again, I smelled cigarette smoke. If there were pregnant women around, somebody needed to let them know about the effects of smoking on their fetuses. Hands pushed a bowl with some kind of thick soup and a cup of clear broth through the slot in the door. In the left hand, wrapped around the cup, was a cigarette still burning. Maybe I could use the lit cigarette as a weapon. Before I could move, the hand and the cigarette disappeared into the food slot.

"Fredricka, is that you?" I needed information about the world outside and about Troy. "What time is it?" Might as well start with the easy stuff.

"A little after seven." The voice sounded like Fredricka's.

I looked at the window, saw only a gray haze. "Morning or night?"

"Morning. This is your breakfast." Followed by the intake of breath.

"Fredricka, are you pregnant?"

"We all are."

"But you're still smoking?"

"Never heard of no baby dying of lung cancer." Footsteps retreated down the hall and a door slammed.

Next time I woke, no headache. Good news: The pills seemed to be ibuprofen and they had worked. Still tired, but not a drugged tired. Bad news: I was afraid my comments about smoking had sent my only source of information away for good.

My best chance at escape was through the door. The window was tiny, and I didn't want to get stuck in it. Probably couldn't even get my head through. So, the door it was. Troy was on the other side, but I had no idea whether he knew where I was. I leaned on the door. It didn't give. I tapped it. It sounded solid, but what did I know about doors? I'd read somewhere about people removing hinges and getting out, but the hinges were on the other side.

Somebody on the outside needed to open the door. Could I ask for something too big to go through the slot? A blanket? It might fit. Or they might just ignore me or tell me to do without.

I looked around the cell again. The toilet. Maybe I could stop up the toilet. This wasn't the city, they probably had a septic system. If there were a lot of toilets, a good chance with all these buildings, they'd need to fix it before it backed up into other places. Or maybe not. Maybe they'd just let me sit in with the sewage. Oh, hell, I didn't have a better plan.

I'd never tried to stop up a toilet before. I'd seen other people do it. Stopping toilets was a favored activity in foster care. But then we had lots of stuff to put down the toilet. Sponges and towels and stuffed animals. All I had was the toilet paper and my jacket. And without my jacket, it was damned cold in the cell. I thought about filling the toilet and then plugging it but that seemed messy and disgusting. So, I pushed the toilet paper roll through the standing water. In the end, I had to use my jacket to get it stopped up good. I flushed the toilet and the water overflowed. It was just water, so no smell, but it was cold, and it picked up junk as it flowed over the floor. On the plus side, it drowned quite a few bugs.

I climbed on the couch and waited. Some of the water flowed under the door and through the food slot, so there was only an inch or two on the floor. But it was cold, and the back of my mouth tasted like stagnant water. Forget about opening the door, nobody showed up at all. It was cold and wet and still gray outside. And now I needed to go to the bathroom.

Tap, tap. Was somebody coming? I yelled and said that the toilet was stopped up. I banged on the door. Standing in the freezing water, I listened for footsteps.

The window over the toilet shattered. Tiny bits of glass fell into the water on the floor.

"Niagara are you there?" The voice, barely a whisper, belonged to Troy.

All I could see was a silhouette against the window.

"Troy?" I waded through the water and climbed up on the toilet seat. I heard a whimper.

"Be quiet." Troy rolled his jacket around his arm and cleared the rest of the glass from the window. "I found my kids. They're with me. We need to get out of here. I'll pull you through the window."

"The window's tiny. I'll never fit."

"Try anyway."

I lifted my arms and Troy grabbed them by the elbows. I attempted to scramble up the cold, slick walls. If we got out of here, I was going to the gym every day.

"Why are you wet?"

"It's the toilet. I clogged it up, hoping somebody'd open the door."

"Good plan." Troy pulled one of my shoulders out of the window.

"But it didn't work." I jammed my body into the window frame. Still only one shoulder fit through. "And it looks like this won't work either."

Troy poked and pulled my head and shoulder. I heard the whimper again, outside the window. The kids weren't going to be quiet much longer. Troy leaned back.

"Okay, let's try it again. This time put both your hands through first and I'll pull you."

I did as Troy asked. I put my arms together, twined my fingers, and pushed through the window. Troy pulled. My arms hurt.

"This isn't working," I let go, slipped, and fell back into the room, hitting my butt on the toilet as I went down.

"Are you alright?" Troy put his head through the window and looked down on me.

"I'll have bruises, but I'm okay," I said. "A little wetter than before, and it's cold."

"I've got to get the kids out of here, before they wake up the whole place." Troy's face disappeared from the window.

I climbed back on the toilet seat and saw him, now holding David.

"Is there another way out of the room?" Troy asked.

"Only the door." I put my hand out the window. "And it's locked."

Troy took my hand. "I could go into the building and open it from the outside."

"Even if you had time, and it wasn't locked, what would you do with the children?"

Troy put down David. It must be getting lighter. I could see them all clearly.

"I don't want to leave without you."

"Daddy, I'm cold," said Debbie. She stamped her feet.

"You've got to get out of here," I said. Please say no, you'll wait for me.

Troy pushed a revolver through the window. It looked like the .38 I had used to shoot LaValley. "Take this," he said.

"I don't want a gun." It fell from the window onto the back of the toilet. I caught it before it fell into the water.

"I hope you won't need to use it," said Troy. "But if you do, don't hesitate."

Debbie was making louder noises.

"I've got to get the kids to safety." Troy turned to go. "I'll be back for you. Soon."

The cold and damp crept into my bones.

He left me there. Locked in a cell with no escape. He had an excellent reason. He needed to take care of his kids. And, if the kids started to make noise, we would all be caught, and nobody knew where we were.

But still I felt abandoned. He picked his kids over me. Just like I would want a good parent to do.

Troy would send help as soon as the kids were safe. Or Jacque might figure it out and send help. I needed to sit and wait. I'm not good at waiting.

He left me here alone.

Good News Conference Center
Deer Lick, Vermont
After Sunrise

I was crying. Hadn't cried in years, but now the tears just kept coming. He left me here. He didn't want to, but his children came first.

And if the children continued to make noise, none of us could escape. I understood that. My rational, logical brain knew that Troy leaving with the children was the best shot for us all to escape. Still, I felt abandoned. Hell, I was abandoned. Alone in a cold, stone cell with six inches of sewer water on the floor. Ugh. And a dead mouse floating in the muck. Where did that come from? A gun I didn't want.

No matter what happened to Troy, he and his children were safe. I did my part to save them, even if I couldn't save my brother. Not save him. I had kicked him away so that I didn't go under with him. Just as Troy kicked me away to save his children.

This is how it felt, being left behind. I stood up. The freezing water swirled around my ankles. If it kept rising, I could drown in freezing, dirty water.

Not today.

Frost formed on the broken window. Frigid air crept into the walls, making my hands hurt when I touched the stones. I climbed back on the toilet seat and attempted to get through the window again. The tiny shards of glass bit into my palms. My lungs stopped momentarily when the wind blew into the cell.

Breathe. Cold and wet, but I needed to breathe. I pulled myself up to the window.

A shard of glass dug into my hand, between the thumb and index finger. In sympathy, the stitches in my leg pulled and itched. Blood flowed down my hand and I lost my grip. My feet contacted the toilet lid and slid into the toilet.

I slid down the bowl and landed on my butt in the muck. Well, at least I hadn't broken a limb or a bone. Though the filthy water didn't do much for the stitches. My lower back hurt where I landed, and I would probably have bruises tomorrow.

If I made it to tomorrow. The water, no matter how filthy, stopped the flow of blood. An infection would be likely. The water was slowly seeping out of the cell, but it still covered the floor.

The door opened with a clang. I stepped back.

"What are you doing?" The woman asking the questions had dirty blond hair, cut short on one side and shaggy on the other. She picked up her feet and examined the wet hems of her jeans.

I remained silent. Didn't know whether it would be better to admit to causing the mess, claim ignorance, or beg her to get me out of here.

"Doesn't matter anyway," she said. "We're out of here."

She reached for me, then pulled her hands away at the last minute. "Niagara, you smell terrible. You take a bath in this stuff?" The voice was Fredricka's, my would-be jailer. "Sorry." Now I was apologizing to her.

Fredricka took hold of my arm and turned to go.

"Where are we going?"

"Order came that we're moving. Pregnant women, children, everybody. Almost ready to go when I remembered you were still down here. Came to get you." Fredricka edged away from the floating mouse. "What did you do here anyway?"

"Toilet's plugged," I said. "Where are we going?"

Fredricka shrugged. "Don't know. We're just told to move. Somebody said out of the country. That might be nice, I've never been anywhere but boring Vermont."

Fredricka didn't seem to be aware that I was a prisoner. She led me out of the cell and down the gray corridor as if she expected me to go with her. I had other ideas.

We came to stone steps that looked like they were carved out of the wall. Fredricka let go of my arm and started up the steps ahead of me. I had nowhere else to go, so I followed her.

We came out in one of the buildings at the compound, not the reception building Troy and I were in before. It was smaller but laid out in the same pattern, with a center hallway and connecting rooms on either side.

We passed one of the rooms and I heard a high-pitched voice. It sounded like General Counsel Damon Davis. Couldn't be. Why would he be in Vermont? Then I heard it again and stood outside the partially opened door.

"We'll need passports to pull that off," he said.

Fredricka pulled on my arm. I took a few steps down the corridor with her.

"Be right back." I kept my voice low. "Got to go to the bathroom before we leave."

"Okay, the bathroom's back at the top of the stairs." Fredricka kept her voice low too.

I wiggled my fingers in goodbye and turned back. Fredricka kept on and went through a door at the end of the corridor.

I looked around. The layout was just like the other building, with connecting doors between the rooms. I slipped into the room next to Davis and leaned on the door. No need to open it; the walls had little insulation and the voices were clear. There were at least two other people with him, a man and a woman.

"There's no time to take everything with us," said the other man.

"Just leave it. Nobody's been in here for months, they'll just think its junk," said the woman.

"Lots of expense to replace everything," said Davis. "We could have taken it all if you'd moved when I told you to."

"But I like it here," said the man. "Didn't want to move. And I tried to take care of the lawyer lady and the rent-a-cop." He sounded familiar, but I couldn't place the voice.

"But you didn't take care of it," said the woman.

"Niagara, where are you?" Fredricka's voice echoed down the hallway. "We can't wait much longer."

Two sets of footsteps left the room and walked into the hallway.

"Why are you looking for Niagara?" said Davis. "Isn't she downstairs?"

"No," said Fredricka, barely above a whisper. "I went down to get her, so she could leave with us."

"How'd you get the key?" High pitched didn't describe Davis's voice now. He was a soprano.

"Lemore showed me where it was." I had to strain to hear Fredricka.

"Lemore, what the hell?!" Davis was bellowing now. Didn't think he had it in him.

"Let's just find her. Now." This from the other man.

While they were talking in the hallway, I looked around the room. It had two plastic chairs, a matted carpet, and a large window overlooking the lake. The window didn't have bars and it was only a few feet off the ground. The only means of escape that didn't take me past the people in the corridor. I jammed the window up and it shuddered and finally let go. Made a hell of a noise, but it couldn't be helped. I was out the window and on the ground before anybody caught me.

The smell of thyme engulfed me. Another garden kept alive through the cold and oncoming snow. I ran.

"Stop!" A head popped out of the window. "Stop her!"

This side of the building faced the lake and was deserted. I heard people talking and a motor running on the other side. I picked the darkest part of the yard and ran toward it.

Lemore Dinsmore came out of the building first, followed by Damon Davis. No sign of the woman leaving the building. But there were at least twenty women and as many children in the yard. They boarded a school bus with "God is Love" painted on the side. Maybe I could blend in and get on the bus.

I stayed in the shadows. Dinsmore knew who I was, but nobody else seemed to pay much attention to me. The loading of the vans and other vehicles was well under way. Not smooth. Too many awkward pregnant women and sleepy children. Most of them got in the vehicles willingly.

I stood against the building and surveyed the compound. The building I stood against was closest to the lake. About a dozen yards from where I was stood a fence with warnings about a steep drop to the water. I had no way of telling how steep a drop or how long; I hadn't paid much attention when we were here in the daylight. The gun pressed against my thigh from the pocket of my jeans. Everyone in the compound would know where I was if I fired it. They'd know soon anyway. The sun was up.

The wind bit into me. Wet jeans clung to my legs, offering little protection.

To my right and behind me stood most of the compound and its buildings. All well-lit and very open. I could use some of the darkness of a few hours ago. To my left was the forest. I didn't know how large or thick it was. Perhaps just a few feet of forest and I would be free. Or maybe it went on for miles.

I edged in the direction of the trees. The woods provided the best cover, no matter how thick. Suppressing an urge to break free, I forced myself to slow down and look at the other people milling around. Waiting for an opening and a chance to run.

I edged further along the side of the building. After the corner, it was only about fifty yards to the woods.

Someone shouted. I walked faster. Almost reaching the end of the building. Two men came from the crowd and started after me. They had jackets and boots and the blowing wind didn't slow them down.

I ran. Freezing. No coat and my shoes and pants were wet from wading through the water in the cell. Wind chill. All New England weather forecasts gave a wind chill factor. This felt like below freezing.

I kept moving. Didn't make me any warmer but at least it gave me the illusion of progress.

Just a few more yards to the woods. I couldn't outrun them but maybe I could lose them. Flashes of the night at the gun club came to me.

I entered the woods, my lungs burning. The ground was uneven, and I groped around in the shadows. My feet made contact with something hard and I went down on my left side. Definitely a bruise tomorrow. If I made it that long. Pine needles made everything slick.

I spied a cluster of bushes, low to the ground. A narrow opening where something much smaller than me had entered the bushes. I pushed through, scratching my arms and getting hit in the face. I squatted on the cold ground and used a branch to try to hide signs of my passing.

The ground was freezing and smelled like mold. My legs and back already ached. But if I moved, the men would spot me. *Don't run, don't run, don't run.*

The men hit the bushes as they talked. I heard one say they needed to find me but didn't get paid enough to tramp around the woods in the freezing cold.

"Want to go back?" the man in brown boots asked.

"No way." Black boots loomed over my hiding place. "The sticks here are broken, like somebody came through here in a hurry."

"Who the hell are you, Daniel Boone?" But his partner shoved him aside and studied the brush above my head.

Do not run.

"We've got to be close." Brown boots started swinging some type of baton or stick. It came within inches of my head. The man stepped closer.

I scurried backward. The thick brush hindered my movements.

"Hey, something's in there. You take that side, I'm going in here."

I stood up and ran. My arms and face stung as I pushed through the underbrush. I felt welts and tasted the metallic tang of blood in my mouth. But I kept running.

Both men started after me. I heard a thud as something hit the tree next to me.

"Damn, I missed."

Two more thuds. At least one of the men had a gun. On television, the heroine counted the bullets to figure out when she was safe. I didn't even know how many bullets were in the gun. And I couldn't shoot my gun and run at the same time. Hell, I wasn't even a good runner.

The cold air filled my lungs. I couldn't feel my feet. I needed another place to hide and catch my breath. Still bleeding. Neither of my pursuers had produced a light, so they were as blind as me. They were following my sound.

This was my last thought before I ran out of the woods onto a stone path. Both men stepped out of the shadows immediately after me. More light here, maybe they could see me. I was on the walk around the lake. Probably silhouetted against the gray granite. I remembered the signs warning of a sharp drop to the lake. How sharp? How far down? I hated water.

On one side, the drop to the lake. On the other side, armed men who probably had some bullets left. I had a gun but still had nightmares about the last time I used it. The water was gray and choppy below me.

I jumped into the lake.

Good News Conference Center
Deer Lick, Vermont
A few minutes later

The water closed over my head. I went down and down and couldn't breathe. Images of Richard flashed in the water. Another time when I couldn't breathe and had to save myself. Other regrets surfaced. I didn't tell Troy how I felt about him. I didn't tell Jacque how much I appreciated him. And I still had questions about what was going on. Hell, I even thought about Alvarez.

It was freezing. Not at all like the summer lake the day Richard died. My jeans weighed me down and I had no idea how deep this lake was. All I wanted to do was breathe.

Then I hit the bottom of the lake, thick with mud and slimy vegetation. The lake wasn't deep here, and I was still alive. If I wanted to make changes in the future, I needed to survive.

I planted my feet firmly on the bottom, despite the mud and the slime. Pushed off with all my strength. Seemed like an eternity, but it was probably only a few seconds before my head was above the water. I gulped the air. Thankful just to breathe.

First problem solved. But now I needed to get out of the lake before hypothermia set in. November in New England; it wouldn't be long before my body couldn't maintain its temperature. And I didn't know where my pursuers were.

My body wasn't shivering. I couldn't remember whether that was good or bad, but I had to get out of here. My arms felt like blocks of wood. They didn't bend, and they just splashed on the surface of the water. My legs gave a few feeble kicks.

It was enough to get me to the shore. No smooth sand beach here. The tiny pebbles scraped against my hands and legs. Now I was shivering. An all-body, bone-shaking shivering.

I heard sirens. Lots of sirens. Then the sound of doors slamming and the red and blue lights flashing across the lake. The cavalry had arrived. I tried to shout but it sounded more like a croak. If I didn't get warm and covered soon, all my efforts would be for nothing.

I didn't hear any gunshots, so at least my pursuers were otherwise occupied.

The gun. It was still in my pocket. Now I had a good use for it. With all sirens and police officers, they would notice a gun shot. I pointed the gun across the lake and pulled the trigger. It was loud, and the gun recoiled in my hand. I held it further away from my body and pulled the trigger again. Good old revolver, no problems shooting it even after my swim. I heard people scrambling down the side of the cliff and shouting before I passed out.

When I came to again, I wasn't shivering. I wasn't warm, but I wasn't shivering. I found myself on a gurney in the conference center parking lot, wrapped in warm blankets. Someone had taken my shirt and jeans, but I wasn't going to quibble about that.

I looked around. Dozens of people, most of them women and children, milled around the parking lot. EMT personnel and three ambulances took care of the wounded. Mostly cuts and scratches and one visibly pregnant woman who seemed to be in labor. Law enforcement officers, sheriff and local police, strutted around looking like they knew what they were doing.

I sat up on the gurney. An EMT person, a blond male who looked about nineteen, took my hand.

"Lie back down," he said. "We need to get you to the hospital."

"No," I said. "I need to talk to somebody in charge." I swung my legs off the gurney.

"You need to lie down." The EMT guy put his hands on my shoulders.

"Not right now." I slid off the side and stood. So far, so good. Shaky, but I was standing up.

A woman dressed in a deputy sheriff's uniform walked by. I stepped in front of her.

Her hand went to her gun. "Can I help you?"

"I just got out of the lake." All my legal schooling and this is the best I can come up with. "I was held captive in the conference center."

"I know," said the deputy. "We'll want to talk to you later. Other things going on now." She took a step back.

"I know you're busy, but there's some things you need to know.

This place buys and sells children. Forged birth certificates, some with my name on them. I didn't do it. Lemore Dinsmore, from Deer Lick, is involved with Damon Davis from Massachusetts. I think Amanda Simmons has a part, too, but I don't know the details."

"We've picked up Dinsmore. Haven't seen the other two." She looked over my head. "Don't know about selling children, but we have enough to make a kidnapping case. Got to run, talk to you later." She was gone.

My entire body shook. Guess the shivering didn't stop.

"Back on the gurney." The EMT took me by the shoulders and made me lie down. "We've got to get you warm."

He put more blankets around me. I fell asleep.

Essex Community Hospital
Essex, Vermont
10:35 AM

I don't remember the ambulance ride, but I woke up with Troy by my side. We were in the emergency room of the local hospital. I was wrapped in blankets that had been in a warmer. An IV ran from the back of my hand.

"How are you feeling?" he asked.

"Much better. I'm warm." I lifted my arm. "What's with this?"

"A precaution." He picked up my hand, the one without an IV. "You tore your stitches with your stunt in the water. Some antibiotics to deal with infection.

"Did they get Davis and the others?"

"They picked up Dinsmore and found evidence of links to Amanda Simmons. Don't know whether they can tie in Davis and any others."

"But Davis was there. I saw him."

"His story is that he heard my kids were at the center and came to get them." Troy let go of my hand. "Not that I believe them."

"What do you mean? How did you get out of there?"

"I left the building after the people took you and started looking for another way in. Heard crying in another building and found my kids. After we found you, I went to the sheriff's station. My story was enough to get a warrant for kidnapping."

"How are your kids?"

"Back in state custody, but at least they're with Jacque. Scared and confused." He sighed. "I'll fill you in on the details when we get out of here."

"When can I get out of here?"

"Any time now. You don't have any clothes. The EMTs cut off your shirt and pants. But I've managed to talk the nurse out of some scrubs." He held up a pair of dusty rose scrubs, with "Essex Community Hospital" across the back.

"Guess they'll have to do." I took the scrubs from him. "Now go get us some coffee while I change."

He left, and I got out of bed. The stitches did look angry, red and inflamed. No discharge and they didn't look infected, but I'm a lawyer, not a doctor. I dragged the IV pole into the bathroom and changed there. Getting the top over my head took most of my energy.

When I came back into my room, a police officer stood there. A woman, about fifty, with short, gray hair and wire-rim glasses.

"Miss Fontaine?" she said.

"Yes, I'm Niagara Fontaine. Can I help you?"

"You spoke to Deputy Lois Divoll earlier this morning. She said I'd be coming by to interview you. Officer Marion Mikolinus." She stood with her legs apart and her arms resting on her belt.

"Yes, I remember Deputy Divoll from the conference center." I sat in the only chair in the room. "Do we have to do this now?"

"We need to go over this information now, when it's fresh in your mind. You're a lawyer, aren't you? If you called me as a witness, you'd expect statements from everyone right after the incident, right?"

"Yes, that's right."

"So, let's go find a place to talk."

"Let's stay here. I'm still hooked up to this IV for a few more minutes."

Troy entered the room with two cups of coffee and stopped short when he saw Officer Mikolinus.

"Officer Mikolinus," he said.

"Mr. Higgins," she replied. "How are your kids doing?"

"Not well." Troy looked her in the eye. "How do you expect them to be doing?"

Officer Mikolinus looked past him to me. "I need to talk to Miss Fontaine. Alone."

Troy handed me my coffee. "I'll go see if there's anything else they need before they discharge you." He looked at the officer. "I'll be back in half an hour."

"Now tell me what happened," she said.

I started at the warning from Alvarez and brought her up to the overheard conversation at the conference center and the chase that led me to the lake.

"So the adoption certificates, allegedly forged, have your name on them." Officer Mikolinus put a stack of papers between us.

"The ones I saw had my name on them. That's why the receptionist from Meredith Mills called me when she found them in the river."

"I'll be checking with her," said the officer.

"Please do," I replied. "I would like to get that cleared up, so you can concentrate on the other matters."

"You do have to admit, Miss Fontaine, that you are connected to a number of people from the center."

"What do you mean, a number of people? Damon Davis is my boss, and I see Amanda Simmons a few times a year."

"We haven't connected them to the conference center," said Mikolinus. "I'm talking about Josie Miller, Troy Higgins' children, and the dead Scarlett Scarletti."

"So Vermont authorities are interested in Massachusetts cases?"

Mikolinus tapped her file. "They do seem to be connected."

It was an effort not to show my feelings on my face.

"You shot Mr. LaValley." Mikolinus cleared the papers from the table. "Were you looking for his child?"

"I shot Mr. LaValley in Massachusetts. I only linked him to the center yesterday. Mr. Higgins and I came looking for his children."

"You and Mr. Higgins are close." It wasn't a question, so I didn't answer.

"Can you tell me why you are involved with so many women and children who have been at the conference center?"

That I could answer. "I'm the attorney for the Department of Children and Families. I encounter thousands of children in my work. All adoptions in Massachusetts must go through an adoption agency, so it is a prime place for selling children and faking paperwork. But you knew that."

Mikolinus adjusted her gun belt. "I did. But you and Higgins seem to be a special target."

"Special target?"

"Yes, somebody blew up the truck you and Higgins were travelling in. Can you explain that?"

"Guess we got closer to the truth than you did." Not exactly fair, but she was getting under my skin.

Troy opened the door, without knocking, and entered the room.

"Guess the half hour is up," I said. "I'm leaving. If you have any other questions, please contact me in Massachusetts."

Mikolinus left, the nurse took out the IV, and Troy and I left the hospital.

Troy and I went to the sheriff's station where his children were being held.

"You smell like dirty water," said Debbie.

"I took a shower at the hospital," I said. My hair still smelled like pond scum. "Maybe I need another one."

Jacque was there too. He had custody of Debbie and David. They fell asleep shortly after we arrived, so his duties were light.

Jacque paced the length of the room—nine strides—turned around and paced back. His phone rang.

"Bro, I got info for you." Amir Burrows, his informant, was talking, and his cheery voice could be heard across the room. "Answers to questions you asked."

Jacque put the phone on speaker and came over to Troy and me.

"Okay, Amir. Got you on speaker. What you got for me?"

"Asked some people, got some answers. Fake papers is big business. Got accountants and everything."

"Amir, you got any information I can use? Like, where do the forged birth certificates come from?"

"From Four Medallions."

"Four what?"

"Medallions. You know, like circles."

Jacque found a piece of paper to take notes. "What have circles got to do with forged birth certificates?"

"Everything, man. Four Medallions is the name of the company does document preparations. Some legit, some not so legit." Amir went on to describe a printing company with invoicing, shipping, and international production of documents. "And everything gets billed to Four Medallions Company. Got their fancy circles logo on every bit of paper. Use the legit stuff to cover the rest."

"Circles logo?"

"Yeah, they got this fancy checkmark-shaped logo. Sure, you seen it. One big circle on the left and three little circles up the side.

Somebody's real proud of it, cause it's on every paper they send out."

Circles. After her sister's death, Amber Scarletti drew circles on paper and on the tabletop. Jacque couldn't get her to stop drawing circles.

"And these circles are on everything?" Jacque asked.

"Yeah." Amir hesitated. "I thought you were interested in figures and documents, not circles." "Didn't think the circles and forgeries were connected until now." Jacque continued to take notes. "Ever hear of a guy named Jimmy Scarletti?"

"Nope. Is he important?"

"Don't know," said Jacque.

The sheriff's deputies returned to the station. Along with a half-dozen pregnant women and a lot of children. The sheriff's deputies, a man and a woman, looked stressed.

"I'm going to call Children and Youth Services," said the male deputy, and he left the room.

The female deputy looked around at the women and children. Took out forms and tried to get the women to fill them out. Everybody ignored her. The children continued to run around the station.

Jacque walked over to the woman. "Can I help, Deputy...?"

"Divoll. Lois Divoll." The woman brought her hand to her mouth, thought better of it, and dropped it to her side. "I could use some help."

Jacque worked his magic. He had the women filling out forms and the children entertained within fifteen minutes. It was still loud, but not chaotic.

"Deputy Divoll," I called. "Can we talk to you?"

She came over to us. "Call me Lois. Sorry, I forgot your names."

"This is Troy Higgins," I said. "I'm Niagara Fontaine, and I'm an attorney for the Massachusetts Department of Children and Families. What's happening now?"

"You're the lady went into the lake." Now she knew who I was. "How are you feeling?"

"I'm clean and warm," I said. "Other than that, I'm mostly

curious about what happened."

"Because of what the two of you saw, we got a warrant to go out to the conference center. Found these women and children and brought them back here. Most of them say they came here to have their babies and get them adopted. That's not illegal in Vermont."

"But it is in Massachusetts," I said.

"Don't enforce Massachusetts law," replied the deputy. "Got enough problems here."

"What about my being held there?"

"Found the room, just like you said." Lois Divoll looked around the room, seemed satisfied by what she saw, and turned back to us. "Picked up a couple of men could be the ones that held and chased you. Other deputies are still out there going through rooms and looking for people left behind. Dinsmore will be questioned, but claims he was only doing transportation."

"So, we just wait and see," I said. Not like in the movies or TV, when everything gets tied up in an hour.

"All we can do," said Divoll.

MONDAY, NOVEMBER 15

Massachusetts Technology Laboratory
Quincy, Massachusetts
11:40 AM

I sat in the Massachusetts State Technology lab and savored the feelings of warmth and comfort. Troy sat next to me now, solid and secure. We were watching a download of the sheriff's department at the conference center.

The picture was uneven and the lighting bad. The police technician, Albert Sulkey, said it was the best he could do. Body cams didn't have great resolution. And we were looking at copies, as Vermont authorities kept the originals.

The clip started with a broad view of the Good News Conference Center.

"When was this recorded?" I tried to make out the tiny letters at the bottom of the screen.

Albert hit a button and the time stamp expanded. "It says 07:43 yesterday. By all accounts, that's pretty accurate."

The sheriff's deputies entered a building with two very pregnant women and a handful of children. A pregnant woman trying to get out of the way. Scenes of screaming children being handed to child welfare workers. The clip ended with a close-up of a dark-haired toddler lisping "mama, mama, mama."

The screen went blank. Albert turned off the monitor. Behind him sat Troy and Lois Divoll, the Vermont deputy sheriff. She was in Massachusetts to sort out the details.

"Looks worse than it was," Divoll said. "We caught up with the vehicles leaving the center. We're still trying to sort out children, get them to the proper homes."

"And what about Davis?" I asked.

"Got him too," said Divoll. "His name is on some of the conference center documents. We can trace the forged adoption certificates to him, though he tried to blame Niagara. Will take some doing, but I think we have a case."

"Where is he now?" I hoped he was rotting in jail.

"He's out on bond," said Divoll. "He was arraigned this morning, according to the Massachusetts troopers, and he made bail. It was high, but he made it."

"Probably paid for by all the illegal adoptions he did." I couldn't keep the bitterness out of my voice. He was scum, and he used my name to do his evil deeds.

"May be," replied Divoll. "It appears that he's been doing it for over twenty years. Don't know how far back they can go, but it's not likely he'll get charged for everything he did."

So much destruction, so many wasted lives. The women and few men at the conference center were charged. Missing children placed in care. The people running the scheme couldn't be traced. They had followed the paper trail to Davis. Maybe he would talk for a deal.

"What about Scarlett Scarletti?" I asked. "How did she fit into all of this?" During the long, cold night, I had not thought of Scarlett at all.

"She knew too much." Troy picked up a folder and opened it. "According to Bella, her mother, Scarlett threatened to tell where they had been and what she had seen. Jimmy wanted Scarlett to get pregnant, sell her baby, and contribute to the family income. She refused, they fought, she died."

"Can they pin that on Davis?" I asked. "Conspiracy maybe."

"That'll be hard to prove," said Troy. "I know it's not enough, but it's the best we can do."

"What about Gary LaValley? The guy I shot?" I continued. "Will he at least spend time in jail?"

"He worked for Medallion Printing. Got the fake paper for Davis and other people. Was afraid you would trace it back to him, so he came after you." Divoll flipped some pages in her folder. "With your testimony, he'll do time."

"And the gunman at the courthouse?"

"Not everything is about you, Niagara." This from Jacque who had just joined us. "Seemed you were just in the wrong place at the wrong time."

"So, that's it?" I leaned back in my chair. "Some bad guys get caught, some don't, and a child is dead. No tidy ending like in the movies."

Troy and Jacque looked at each other. Troy couldn't maintain eye contact.

"What else is there?" I looked from Troy to Jacque and back. "What aren't you telling me?"

Divoll tapped Albert on the shoulder. "C'mon fella, this is where we leave." Divoll, Jacque, and Albert left.

Troy and I were alone in the room. Troy picked up another file folder.

"There were records at the conference center going back twenty or thirty years." He placed the folder in front of me. "Probably the scheme was even more profitable back then, when all adoptions went through an agency."

I looked at the file in front of me. The tab on the side said "Fontaine, Richard, dob 8/13/1989."

My brother. It was my brother's file. I picked it up. "Where did you get this?"

"At the conference center. In the adoption files."

"Adoption files? My brother wasn't adopted. I remember him being born. I was only four years old, but I remember visiting him and my mother in the hospital. Back then my dad had to sneak me in."

"Ricky was adopted later."

"Later? When later? Ricky died a week before his second birthday."

Troy put his hand on my shoulder. "What do you remember about the day he died?"

I swallowed. I didn't want to remember.

"Please," said Troy. "It's important."

"It was the worst day of my life." I stood up. "I don't want to talk about it."

Troy didn't move.

"My parents took us to the lake," I continued, despite my reluctance. "Ricky and I went in the water. My parents were involved with each other, not watching us. Ricky went under. I tried to save him."

"How old were you?"

"Six. But everybody said I was a big girl. My parents were so into each other, they didn't pay much attention to Ricky and me. I made him cereal, prepared bottles, played with him." I picked up a pen from the desk. "I thought I could pull him out."

"But you couldn't."

"No, he pulled me under. I thought I was going to drown too. I pushed him aside to get to the beach. He never came back up." I found I had no tears left.

Troy stepped up to me and embraced me in a bear hug.

"Then what happened?" Troy held me closer.

"Ricky died. I went into foster care because my parents didn't watch me. Never saw Ricky or my parents again."

"Never again?"

"My parents died in a car crash right after I went into foster care. Temporary care became permanent."

Troy held on. He smelled like wool and aftershave. Good, comforting smells. I took a deep breath and backed away from him.

"Niagara, Ricky may not have died that day. That's what's in the folder." Troy picked it up again. "Damon Davis was a social worker back then. He may have arranged for Ricky to be adopted."

I don't often do "what if?" but the thoughts ran through my head. What if I had been raised with Ricky? What if we had stayed together? What did Ricky look like now?

"Ricky is alive? He came out of the pond? I have a family?" I realized I was babbling.

I'd been alone all these years. It was a cruel joke.

"I don't know. Ricky appears to have been alive after the alleged drowning, but we don't know where he is or if he is alive now. There's no record of him after 1994." Troy stepped closer.

"But we need to look for him. What if something bad happened to him?"

"Niagara, we just don't know." Troy put his arm around me.

I found I still had some tears left. For all the missed chances.

"I missed my chance at a family," I said.

"But you have a family. You have me, and my children, if you want them. We'll be your family. And, if you want to, we'll help you look for Ricky."

I can do that. Perseverance is my strongest trait.

ACKNOWLEDGMENTS

First, thank you to all my readers, especially those who read the acknowledgements. Without you, I would be just a crazy woman making up stories. With you, I am an author.

Many, many thanks to all the men and women who work every day in the child welfare system. It's tough work and most of you do it with dedication and determination. I learned lessons in life and work from the attorneys I worked with including Jan Najemy, Fran Yee, Roy Montoya, Ellen Cain and Deirdre Kelleher.

A special thanks to George Comeaux, Ann Forcier, Valerie Lane, Gwenn Meredith, and Loretta Worters who read the manuscript and gave me valuable feedback. I thanked you in alphabetical order to avoid any favoritism. .

My family stood by me as I attempted my first book. Thanks to my late father, William McIntosh, who made me believe I could do anything; to my mother, Marilyn McIntosh, who constantly asked me when I was going to finish the book; and to my sister, Sandy Knight, who encouraged me. I also appreciate the efforts of my nieces, Stormi Knight (yes, that's the name on the birth certificate) who designed my website and Elli Knight who showed me that it's good to take chances.

My son, Tony McIntosh, expressed doubts about this undertaking but his wife, Tina, straightened him out. An extraordinary thanks to the grands, Alexander, Abbigayle, and Brent, to whom this book is dedicated.

NOTICE TO READERS

A FAVOR, PLEASE?

Before you leave this book, would you take a minute and leave a review on Amazon and any other social media that you frequent?

Reviews are very important to me and other authors so, if you like a book, or want to recommend a book, please do a good deed and review it. This allows me and other authors to get more sales and that encourages us to write more books for you to read.

Thanks for your time and attention.

Future Books in Meredith, Massachusetts series

COMING SOON
A.B. HARTWELL
a Meredith, Massachusetts novel

JESUS GABRIEL LEARY
a Meredith, Massachusetts novel

RICHARD FONTAINE
a Meredith, Massachusetts novel

Learn more about upcoming books, giveaways, and first liners at:

jamcintosh.com

ABOUT THE AUTHOR

Photo by Celestial Studios

J. A. McIntosh spent too many years as an attorney for the Commonwealth of Massachusetts, Department of Children and Families, wishing that she was an author. She now spends her time staring out the window, pretending to write, taking walks in the woods, and she has recently started karate classes for no apparent reason. Her son, Tony, says he does not want to be a lawyer or a writer.

Contact her at:
    jamcintosh.com
    jamcintoshesq@gmail.com
    or on her Facebook or Amazon page

www.ingramcontent.com/pod-product-compliance
Lightning Source LLC
Chambersburg PA
CBHW051945220626
47052CB00004B/806